Three Gems

Three Gems

A Celebration of Abilities

DEREK LIANG

PARTRIDGE

To order additional copies of this book, contact
Toll Free 800 101 2657 (Singapore)
Toll Free 1 800 81 7340 (Malaysia)
orders.singapore@partridgepublishing.com

www.partridgepublishing.com/singapore

CONTENTS

ENDORSEMENTS

"Three Gems beautifully narrates the challenges faced by three adolescents with special needs, the private anguish of their families, and the personal growth of their volunteers. It is a celebration of hope and resilience, as well as a nod to kindness, volunteering and support services. We all have the same aspirations, and see the same sun – many who are disadvantaged ask only for equal opportunities and understanding. *Three Gems* is a clarion call for those who may now be feeling down to step out, step up and want more; and for society to open its heart, to give and also expect more."

—Dr Lynne Lim, Senior ENT (Ear, Nose and Throat) Consultant

"Having first started as a volunteer myself, I can see that this book clearly reflects the sacrificial love and relentless pursuit that are needed when following up on a beneficiary. The book also give us insights into the inner feelings of beneficiaries and show us how they eventually overcome the difficulties in their own lives. Inspiring."

—Adeline Wong, Family Care Lead, Prison Fellowship Singapore

"What is the world of silence like, when you are in a world that never stops talking? Derek has managed to capture the real meaning of deafness and the deaf identity as portrayed by Joanne in the book. Insightful and wide-ranging."

—Ong Shi Yi, Senior Executive with Hearing Impairment.

"In a time when #YOLO ("You Only Live Once") and the term "strawberry generation" are commonly associated with my generation, it is refreshing to know of a community of devoted and selfless youth volunteers. Instead of chasing their own dreams and caught up in the rat race and pleasure lifestyle, they are willing to slow down to walk alongside others in need of help, and in turn achieve the #YOLO moment in their journey.

In this book, Derek has perceptively captured the challenges, emotions and sacrifices that volunteers and beneficiaries experience. He has given an insight of the anonymous volunteering scene. My greatest pleasure in reading *Three Gems* is knowing that the good done by the fictional characters is, in fact, real. Highly recommended for those who wish to have their #faithinhumanityrestored, and be inspired to bring out the hidden volunteer inside all of us."

—Eugene Nai, MINDS MYG Chairperson

ACKNOWLEDGEMENT

To my wife, Lynne, for her understanding during those moments when my heart had to go to *Three Gems*. Also thanks to her for sharing her passionate opinion as a fellow volunteer for the deaf, and presenting a different viewpoint from mine, hence making my arguments in this book more multi-faceted.

I am also grateful to the following persons for their sharing, inputs and inspirations which contribute to the writing of the book. Of course, if there are any errors, omissions and oversights, they are mine alone.

To Ms Ong Shiyi, my deaf ex-student who gladly took part in my interviews.

To Ms Bernice Dass and her staff from MINDS-SIA EDC for granting me a visit to the centre and sharing her wealth of experience, without which my research would be incomplete.

To my trainees at Tampines Home (Thomson), Jurong Gardens School, my deaf clients, and my boy at Singapore Boys' Home, all of whom provided the sources of inspiration to make *Three Gems* come true.

To my fellow volunteers, past and present, from Interact Club (Social Service), National Junior College, Welfare Services Club's RSPs (Regular Service Projects) from Nanyang Technological University,

Singapore Association for the Deaf, and MINDS Youth Group's West End Project. They convinced me that *esprit de volontaire* exists, and that each of us can make a difference to the less fortunate.

To Alvan, for believing in *Three Gems* and your faithful editorial work. Without you, the manuscript of this book would have stayed buried in my hard disk drive.

To my beloved younger sister, Weiling (*de.*), who was the reason I took my first step to become a volunteer. This book is dedicated to you.

Finally, to my heavenly Father and Jesus Christ, whose grace and love allows me to complete what He has nudged me to start twelve years ago.

Author's Note

Three Gems was conceived when the National Council of Social Services (NCSS) had embarked on its first-ever, nationwide disability awareness week campaign in November 2004, themed *A Celebration of Abilities*. Among its many objectives that included portraying the abilities of persons with disability and promoting interaction between the public and the disabled, *A Celebration of Abilities* committed to raise public awareness of the disabled in local settings and educating people to accept disability in our lives. I applauded the good intentions behind this project although, in my opinion, it was some ten years overdue.

A survey commissioned by NCSS at the time reported that half of the respondents chose to keep their distance from their disabled counterparts, and the portion of those willing to know more about them was even lower. The campaign garnered the media and the various Voluntary Welfare Organisations (VWOs) together to propagate this awareness. *A Celebration of Abilities* was a small step towards a big cause. It was against this background that I resolved to do my bit towards raising the public awareness of the disadvantaged and disabled in Singapore.

Three Gems tells the tales of three adolescents: a deaf girl, an intellectually disabled boy and a delinquent youth, so like each and every one of us, but in their own ways, rejected by society and mostly forgotten. It portrays the struggles, the dilemmas and hopes carried by each of them and their families, and the roles the respective VWO played in reintegrating them into society. It describes the selfless efforts and experiences of volunteering, and peers deeply into the emotions of the volunteers.

Three Gems is a work of fiction with a mission to depict Singapore's disability scene. It is inspired by real characters and events. However, names, incidents and events in this book are fictitious. Any resemblance to actual persons, living or dead, or actual events is purely coincidental. Finally, through this book, I wish to pay tribute to all the quiet volunteers who have striven hard to give but been reserved to take. The success of *Three Gems*, if any, belongs solely to them.

Derek Liang
9 September 2004

FOREWORD

I have had the pleasure and honour of knowing Derek over the past decade or so. Back in 2007, we were fellow volunteers involved in organising the Deafinitely Boleh Carnival under the auspices of the Singapore Association for the Deaf (SADeaf). Back then, he was just one among many volunteers I encountered during my own stint in the social service and special education field spanning 15 years. But Derek turned out to be that bit different from most others.

It was only much later, upon reading the draft manuscript of the book you are holding now, that I realised the sheer range and depth of his voluntary tour of duty. From his university days onwards, Derek has given his time, effort and expertise to the special needs community in a diverse range of roles and with different welfare organisations in Singapore. Derek was a befriender with youth residents at the Singapore Boys' Home, organised activities for and worked directly with persons with intellectual disability at MINDS (Movement for the Intellectually Disabled of Singapore), and gave tuition to deaf and hard-of-hearing students with his school (Nanyang Technological University) as well as helped in projects with SADeaf.

This account of volunteering with often neglected, misunderstood and underserved groups, based on Derek's real-life experiences, is an engaging one. It is also an important one which offers insights into their respective worlds, and shows the universality of the human experience in spite of all the outwardly superficial differences among us. From his vantage as a veteran volunteer, Derek also offers something novel – a rarely articulated and honest look at the ups and downs, as well as joys and disappointments, of the practical aspects and emotional journey of volunteering.

As a person, Derek has that quality of treating as equals those he worked with, and he is never patronising or condescending. Instead, he consciously tossed aside stereotypes, made the effort to see the bigger picture and delved into the smaller but equally crucial personal details – the unique circumstances, backgrounds and personal stories of the people he interacted. By showing how volunteering benefits the giver as much as the recipient, I hope Derek's book inspires more to step forth and contribute to worthy causes. In its own quiet way, this book also pays a heartfelt tribute to all the volunteers out there who have been selflessly doing crucial work for little recognition and reward.

Lastly, I am proud to know Derek as a friend, a fellow volunteer, and – most of all – as a big-hearted person who serves others with respect and compassion.

Alvan Yap

First Bonds

"We can do no great things, only small things with great love."

Mother Teresa

ABOUT A PAIR

Nobody who had seen Rachel Khoo and Colin Lee together would think they were a couple. Colin was in his usual get-up – an old tee with the letters 'RSP (ID)' embossed across the back and a pair of wrinkled shorts. His hair was unkempt and he sported a stubby, untrimmed beard which seemed to make him look ten years older.

Rachel was way more trendy in her favourite pink lycra blouse, which was tucked into silvery grey drawn pants with a brown velvet belt around her slim waist. Her past sales-related jobs had influenced her sartorial taste. She thought: *Had he ever wondered what image people would form of RSP (ID) if they even knew what it stood for, and of him?* After all, they were at Orchard Road where the fashionistas congregate and where dressing up was mandatory. And it was about the hundredth time she had told him this.

At that point, Rachel was almost resigned to the point of forcing herself to disregard his dowdy dressing. But she was still unhappy and was brooding over it until they started talking. And she was reminded, again, why she chose to be with him. It definitely wasn't for his fashion sense. Seated across a round table at Starbucks, lattes in hand, they updated each other on their happenings.

"So how's Joanne?"

This elicited a big smile from Rachel.

"Oh, I haven't told you ah. She's fine. In fact, on cloud nine now. She'd gotten her A-level results just yesterday and did remarkably well for her GP. She got an A1!" Rachel was beaming as she continued, "For a girl who could not hear the spoken language, her results certainly gives her English teacher, maybe even Beethoven, a run for their money!"

At this, Colin raised an eyebrow. *Oh well, she's exaggerating. But I understand why she's so proud of Joanne.*

Rachel was musing, "You know, Joanne is a very smart girl. But in junior college, she had an inferior complex issue. As if it wasn't hard enough being deaf, having unhelpful classmates and tutors made things worse. I'm just happy I had the chance to be her tutor and to help her along. Now she's done so well!"

"But… but there's a problem. The silly girl does not wish to go on to the U to do engineering. She's made up her mind to quit school and start working. She said she had enough of studying. That can't be true, we're all sure. She doesn't mean it."

"Well, considering her lousy experience at JC, I'm not surprised if it's an excuse," Colin said. "It may be good she wants to take a breather. She's old enough to decide for herself."

Spare me that accusing tone, Rachel thought, beginning to get frustrated. *But what Colin said make loads of sense. Joanne was academically gifted and it would be a pity if she did not go on to university and then a satisfying career. The prestige that came with it would have boosted her self-esteem and served her well in life. She might have had a terrible sort of school life before, but the eventual reward from persevering despite such difficulties must surely be sweet.*

"As her mentor and friend, it's my duty to guide her, right? I'll speak to her again, help her weigh the pros and cons. She's only eighteen and need others' advice. Such a decision shouldn't be made lightly."

"Yah, it's not easy even for a twenty-seven-year-old chap," Colin said, referring to himself.

Rachel ignored Colin's remark. She sipped her decaf, then slowly put the cup down. Her mind was ten thousand miles away; she had started formulating a plan.

———◇———

From behind, Tim Mei watched her elder brother hold their father's hand. Occasionally, Tim Soon leaned his head against Mr Foo as they sauntered down Marina Promenade. They were going to a carnival. It was Sunday, Mr Foo's only day off work. Mrs Foo was by their side, silently matching their pace, enjoying the chatter between father and son. The bright sun and fluffy clouds seemed to reflect the warmness of the Foos' family bond. But not for Tim Mei. She was dragging her feet some distance behind them.

It's so embarrassing, Tim Mei thought. *Bro is already eighteen years old and looks his age. What is Pa thinking of holding his hand in public? Even when I was younger, I didn't let Ma or Pa hold my hand anymore; my friends would have teased me!*

Tim Mei continued to fume silently. Ok, she admitted her brother had been pretty 'normal' – after all, he had learnt to take a bus down to Jurong Gardens School where he studied; he knew how to buy packed dinner for the family when Ma didn't cook; and he was able to do the chores that even Tim Mei felt was beyond her own ability, like washing the toilet and folding the heavy wool blankets and bedsheets. But right now, he was obviously not acting 'normal'.

They passed by the rows of al fresco stalls selling finger food, household gadgets and handphone accessories. "Pa, I want candy." Tim Soon pointed at a rickety stall with a machine that spun out pinkish cotton wool-like threads. Mr Foo gave an approving nod and fished out a two-dollar note from his pocket and placed it onto Tim Soon's palm. The boy skipped towards the stall.

Tim Mei watched him. To the unseasoned eye, Tim Soon's small frame and smooth face belied his real age. But anyone who gave him more than a passing glance would notice his broad shoulders and other signs he was no longer a child. As she watched the transaction between Tim Soon and the hawker, she was also reminded of their childhood days when she had played big sister to her rather dependent elder brother. Then they had gone to the same school at first (before Tim Soon was officially diagnosed), and Tim Mei found herself being mocked at for having a brother with an intellectual disability. She felt hurt at first, but the unkind words slid off her mind when she got home and played with her brother.

Things started to change, though, when the siblings reached their teens. The disparity between their intellectual and language levels became a barrier between them. They were like trains which no longer run on parallel tracks, but had diverged so widely that they stopped calling at the same stations. Slowly, she felt she could not understand him and the way he swung between behaving like an adult and a child, as if he had no control over his own mind and behaviour.

"Uncle, how much is it?"

"It's eighty cents for a stick."

Tim Soon handed the note to him. The hawker held out a stick of candy floss. "Here's your change – one dollar and twenty cents." The hawker seemed to be aware of Tim Soon's condition and spoke to him gently, as if to a young child.

To his surprise, Tim Soon did not immediately take the floss stick, instead clasping the coins in his palm and picking them up, one by one, with his other hand. "Ten cents, fifty cents, eighty cents, one dollar, one dollar and twenty cents." When he was done, he flashed a grin – as if congratulating himself for a job well done – and said to the hawker, "Thank you, uncle." Only then did he collect the candy floss and skipped back to his parents.

Tim Mei took in the scene, impressed in spite of herself. She was surprised her brother could actually count change. It was one of those adult-like moments again, right after he was behaving like a small kid mere minutes ago. She realised that what she lacked was not only an understanding of Tim Soon's thinking, but also of his abilities.

So much have changed between us.

INMATE

"What was the one thing that has been most detrimental to your life?"

Daniel Lok stood at the cookhouse, waiting to collect his food and listening to the radio DJ pose the topic of the day. The call-ins coughed up various answers, some quite serious, while others sounded frivolous or lighthearted: Smoking, drugs, television, mother-in-laws. Daniel let out a snort at the last one. The radio host probed, "So tell us. What did your mother-in-law do to you?"

Daniel emitted another snort. *What was the point of answering that? Fancy an adult complaining to the world about this. And.. detrimental? Does this chap even know what it means? No,* he thought, *mother-in-laws do not abuse you or land you in jail.*

"You there! Stop daydreaming and move!" One of the cooks was yelling at him. Oh, he was holding up the queue. *Asshole.* Daniel cursed under his breath. He looked at the menu – nasi lemak, sambal chilli, ikan bilis, fried egg and cucumber. This wasn't their lucky day though – no fried chicken wings or otah. The rice, thumped onto his plate, was soggy and cooked with what seemed to be spoilt coconut milk. The boy in front of Daniel asked for a little more chilli, and the stony-faced cook deliberately slammed a huge chunk of it on top of his rice. He looked at his ruined lunch and then at the cook as if to protest, only to receive a withering glare, and quietly moved on. *Must be green,* Daniel thought. The food was far from appetising, but it suited him fine and he actually regarded the trice-daily visits to the cookhouse as the highlight of his daily routine.

But, and this might come as a surprise, Daniel was not someone who hankered after good food. Meals at home had been a problem as far back as he could recall, not because his family was poor – on the contrary, they were quite well-to-do – but rather, stocking up on food or preparing meals were not among the tasks on his mother's to-do list. Her gambling addiction had taken over her mind. Nor did Daniel have fond recollections of his businessman father, what with his promiscuity and prolonged absences. During his infrequent appearances, he was aloof from his son and wife.

One day, when he was six, his father stormed into the house and had a big fight with his mother. There were much shouting, accusations, hurled plates and bowls, and, worst of all, a brutal beating. Then he left, for good. Daniel and his mother never saw him again, nor the family savings which vanished with him. His mother was forced to make a living as a seamstress, but whatever she earned was lost at various mahjong tables. She grew increasingly hateful of Daniel, whom she felt was a reminder of her estranged husband. When she lost heavily at gambling, she would come home and vent her rage upon the boy with her fists and a sturdy cane. That was his childhood – fraught with violence, deprivation and absent or abusive parents. As a result, he felt the basic provisions he received here suited him fine, to the puzzlement of many of his fellow inmates.

Daniel walked to the end of the long bench. Two rows in front stood the staff table, where rehabilitation officers, wardens and home administrators had their meals. Daniel saw his assigned Rehabilitation Officer (RO) Mr Tan and Mrs Malathi, the Head of his block, looking serious and deep in conversation. *What's up?* Daniel thought his RO was a nice adult and liked him, though he was careful not to reveal this to his mates.

"Excited about tonight's programme huh?" Lee, who was beside him, piped up. Daniel didn't know his full name, just his nickname 'Butt' – because of the elaborate tattoo of a green dragon and white tiger on his posterior. Every boy was given a nickname. Wee Kiang was 'The Scholar' because of his academic background.

"Nah, not sure if it is a good thing yet."

"You may be right. Look at Mr Tan and the Head there whispering. I smell a plot." Butt was suspicious.

Daniel didn't like Butt, much less such speculations. He did not reply and instead walked off to the basin to wash his tray. Butt was left scowling at being brushed off.

"Enjoy your night, Thief." Butt yelled after him, a hint of menace in his voice.

When Daniel was eight, he thought he had stumbled upon his big break. A famous swimming coach spotted his talent during the school's annual swim meet and signed him up for his own team.

Daniel was soon training at the pool in Toa Payoh every Monday, Wednesday and Friday with a bunch of swimming prodigies. His teammates Mark, Tommy and Fred were consummate swimmers like him. It was a wonderful time for Daniel. By the time they were eleven, they had made their mark at various tournaments and meets, including winning a pair of golds at the Interschool Open, as well as silvers and a bronze at the National Junior Meet.

But while Daniel was accumulating medals, his grades were tumbling downhill. He barely scraped past his academic examinations and, by the following year, he had notched a number of warning letters from his form teacher. Daniel understood why, or at least he thought he did. *It was like the law of conservation of energy. You had only 24 hours per day, so the time and energy you spent on one thing surely means other things, like studies and homework, had to be sacrificed.* His mother could not be bothered about the situation, and nor could Daniel. To him, swimming was everything. His passion for the sport even transcended winning medals or competitions. He just wanted to be in the water, where he felt most free and at peace with himself.

Then came the life-changing incident, out of the blue, when Daniel was twelve. One day at the training pool, Daniel entered his usual cubicle in the changing room after his usual swim practice. He found a bag there, on the ledge behind the shower head. Naturally, he opened it and saw.. bundles of fifty-dollar notes. With shaking hands, he counted the cash. There was five thousand dollars worth of notes in there!

He agonised over it for twenty minutes, pacing around in the cubicle, before he finally came to a decision. *Well, it's my lucky day. Just act normal. Don't mess it up.* He stuffed the cash in his bag, quickly showered, and stepped out of the cubicle. There, his coach was waiting. So was Mark. Mark! What was he doing there? Despite his own shock and fear at being caught in that situation, Daniel still noticed how eerily calm Mark seemed then, his gaze far away and his face expressionless.

The rest was history, as they say. Daniel was accused of theft and, to his astonishment, convicted based on Mark's testimony that he had seen Daniel take the money from the coach's office drawer. The frame-up was what hurt and haunted him most. Why did Mark do that to him? Daniel never had a chance to talk to him though. He was subsequently tried in a Subordinate Court, and sentenced to a three-year stint in the Singapore Boys' Home.

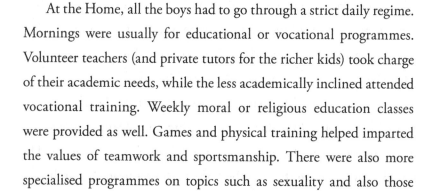

At the Home, all the boys had to go through a strict daily regime. Mornings were usually for educational or vocational programmes. Volunteer teachers (and private tutors for the richer kids) took charge of their academic needs, while the less academically inclined attended vocational training. Weekly moral or religious education classes were provided as well. Games and physical training helped imparted the values of teamwork and sportsmanship. There were also more specialised programmes on topics such as sexuality and also those tailored for residents with special needs such as intellectual disability. But, as far as Daniel knew, Block E had none of these.

That day, after lunch, the RO came in and announced that everyone was to to muster at the square in ten minutes' time for a Basic Life Skills programme. Butt had mentioned there was to be a culinary session. Daniel thought, *Interesting but for what? Did the Home really expect them to cook for themselves after they were discharged?* He was to change his mind soon enough – the class was a lot of fun, and Daniel enjoyed the experience of cooking like a real chef. The boys managed to whip up a western-style chicken chop dish, complete with baked potato and steamed broccoli.

At four o'clock, the boys, for the fourth time that day, mustered at the square. Ball games were a perennial favourite. That was pretty much what an average day consisted of: studying, eating, enrichment activities, playing, and then eating again. *Not too different from life outside*, Daniel mused. But swimming wasn't on the menu because the Home did not have a pool, and that irked Daniel.

Daniel also had problems relating to his peers at the Home. He felt it was because he was different from them – he had not been a street hoodlum or school ruffian. In fact, he was innocent! He made some truly rewarding friendships though – such as with Chua Wee Kiang, his best mate in the block, who had allegedly participated in a riot. Wee Kiang did not fit Daniel's impression of a rioter though. Wee Kiang was quiet, reserved and learned, more like a studious mugger than a streetwise hooligan. He had once confided in Daniel that he had fallen in with bad company after being neglected by his parents.

During weekly family visit sessions, he could see that none of his bunkmates were thrilled or even the slightest bit excited about meeting their families. He thought it was because irresponsible parents, like his own, were the main cause of the boys ending up at the Home. *Why do they bother to come to visit at all? They might as well call those days Weekly Repentance Day. Or Save-Face Day.*

Daniel was particularly put off by the fact that though the staff were caring and responsible types, all they ever preached was diligence and blind obedience to what he regarded as silly rules. They could not see that he could not care less about their rules, and what he needed was just two things: swimming and someone about his age whom he could look up to.

Daniel hoped the newly assigned volunteer befriender he would be meeting that evening would last longer than the previous two.

PRIORITY

A *nd I thought that because deafness is a hidden disability, it means the* *deaf are the most fortunate among the unfortunates,* Colin thought on the way home. *About as hidden as my thoughts in my head. Imagine if Rachel knew what I am thinking.* Behind the windows, the only sound he heard throughout the drive was the hissing of the air-conditioner. Colin stole a glance at his silent girlfriend.

Through much of his adolescence, Colin had intimate knowledge of volunteering. For six or seven years, once a week, he did his bit to add some joy and colour to the lives of those with intellectual disability. Colin had once read that an estimated three out of every hundred babies born had some form of intellectual disability. Colin knew this was obviously inaccurate. Intellectual disability, strictly speaking, refers to below-average intellectual functioning and impairment in adaptive functioning such as communication, learning and self-care. The onset must also be before the age of eighteen. Intellectual disability stems from either congenital or post-natal factors, but the most common causes, particularly in developed countries, occurred after birth.

This much he knew about intellectual disability when he started to volunteer at Tampines Home, Chao Yang Special School and Jurong Gardens School, establishments that could be called homes and schools only to imply familiarity for a group of persons with special needs. At least Tim Soon was, to him, different not so much because of his disability, but because of the big smile he put on for Colin every now and then. As a result of their adaptive functioning impairment, many persons with intellectual disability have slurred speech and limited fine sensory motor skills. And because the manifestation of intellectual disability-related symptoms was varied and unpredictable, the ill-informed would use provocative and demeaning synonyms such as 'mentally sick', 'brain damaged', 'idiot' (Colin would lash out at those who used this particular word) and 'spastic' to describe them.

The media were no help either. They even used phrases like 'deaf and dumb' instead of 'deaf', and 'able-bodied' as an antonym for 'disabled', instead of the proper term 'non-disabled'. Colin did not need to be a language teacher to understand that words were critical in shaping perceptions and attitudes, and using incorrect words could reinforce existing prejudices and misconceptions.

But if persons with intellectual disability were pointy-eared invaders from Mars – which they could not possibly be because, in Colin's view, they were the most innocent and adorable Earthlings – then deaf people would be a race of silent humanoid aliens who heard no voices, but always managed to seamlessly blend into the human race, as though sound was not a necessity in this world. Deafness was a sensory disability, similar to those with visual challenges, but much less apparent. Even his three-year-old nephew couldn't spot a deaf person walking along Millenia Walk among other shoppers, could he?

Unless he went up to strike up a conversation or caught a glimpse of the hearing aids. *Hidden disability indeed.*

Or so Colin realised a long, long time ago. Joanne's decision not to go on to university lingered in his mind. He thought, *Joanne wasn't exactly fortunate to be just deaf. Ironically, she was unfortunate because she was not intellectually disabled and was therefore able to comprehend the implications of her disability – and nothing could be worse than knowing you were being discriminated against, right? On the other hand, those with intellectual disability knew not their limitations, but only their inner strengths, which they will surely need to muster to face their daily challenges. They simply welcome every day of their life with a big smile. Perhaps God had diminished their intellect, but in exchange, He granted them an inherent cheeriness of mind. Heaven's fair after all.*

The car turned into the carpark adjoining his Boon Lay block, where he lived with his parents and, until twelve months ago, his elder brother Lawrence. He suspected that Lawrence must be a bright white star in his previous life for, upon moving out after his marriage, the house became visibly gloomier and more silent. Rachel and Colin took the lift to the eleventh floor and proceeded towards Colin's four-room flat.

The elder Lees were seated on the sofa watching TV. Mr Lee said, "Hi, Rachel, come in."

"Hello, Uncle and Auntie. So sorry to disturb."

"Oh, don't feel that way." This was Mrs Lee. "So have you had your dinner?"

"Yes, we had before we came." Rachel knew the Lees usually had dinner early, and a glance at her watch told her it was already eight, so that could only meant the Lees already had theirs too. But still, respect for elders demanded reciprocity, which also meant you had to ask the obvious. "How about you?" She tried to make it sounded sincere.

"Must be getting ready for supper soon," Colin interrupted teasingly. Rachel shot him a disapproving glance.

Mr Lee chuckled. "He's right. We've already eaten. That's nice of you to ask. Come, take a seat."

The man had stood when receiving his soon-to-be daughter-in-law. A gesture, Colin thought, that encapsulated his father's well-known reputation for hospitality. After they took their positions next to him, he sat down himself, slowly and painfully. For a man of sixty, Colin's father had pretty good health. Except for high blood pressure and mild diabetics, which robbed him of his strength in his lower limbs, he possessed an excellent appetite, a rotund body and an equally rotund face with a natural pinkish glow.

"How's your leg been, Uncle?"

"As usual. It's an old folk's illness. But I can still cycle five kilometres with this pair of useless legs." It was true. He cycled to a nearby market every morning for breakfast and to meet his friends at the coffeeshop to chitchat.

"They are certainly not useless. But try to avoid sweet stuff and you'll be as fine as the day."

That was so Rachel, Colin thought, always playing the concerned guardian role – never mind that his father was more than double her age – and never failing to add a gentle reminder, sometimes a telling off, at the slightest opportunity. *But it is good that your girlfriend cares for your parents, wasn't it?*

"Yah, yah. So how's your work lately?"

A standard question called for a standard answer. Rachel briefly commented on her day. She was an auditory verbal therapist, a job title so rarely encountered that hardly anyone would have heard of it. Most people confused it with that of a speech therapist, as Colin's parents initially did. When people asked, Rachel found that the easiest way to explain her job was to sum it up in one sentence: A speech therapist works with patients in rehabilitating their speech production; while an auditory verbal therapist works with hearing-impaired people, especially with children, and helps them to listen with their hearing aids or cochlear implants.

Mr Lee did not understand anything about cochlear implants or the difference between the two vocations, despite Rachel's enthusiastic explanation, but he could always catch her mood. "That sounds tough. But it's more important that you enjoy what you're doing."

"Yeah! It was kinda challenging. The work hours may be long, but they slip past you when the kids start listening intently and voicing out to you. Really amazing! It's also the kind of job where you get paid to play with toddlers."

"Yah, that is true. So when is the two of you getting married?"

Rachel nearly choked at this twist in the conversation.

Colin quickly came in, "Dad, we do not wish to rush into marriage. We've just started out in our careers."

"You can manage both, I'm sure." This was Mrs Lee, sounding almost exasperated.

"Mum, we both have our careers to think about now. For goodness' sake, Rachel's still under probation and I've just worked for two years with my company. Marriage can wait."

Truth be told, Colin did not mean what he'd just said. Yes, he had a good career laid out before him in the air force and had every intention to give his utmost at work. But he did agree with his mum that having a deep commitment to both career and family were not mutually exclusive; in fact, success in both stemmed from the same desire to make things work out. This explains great corporate and political leaders who were, more often than not, great fathers and husbands. Colin didn't have the intention to become a political or business heavyweight, but in all seriousness, he *did* want to settle down with Rachel as soon as they feasibly could, quite to her annoyance. They had discussed this dozens of times and he knew Rachel expected him to deflect his parents' queries that way.

"Besides, we really hope to save more money to be comfortable…"

"Why haven't you spoken a word since leaving the house?"

It was ten o'clock. Colin and Rachel were cruising along the Pan-Island Expressway, the car windows cranked down slightly. It was a cool November night, the air fresh and not so humid. But Colin's heart was heavy. He could not understand why Rachel was giving him the silent treatment.

"Say something, wouldn't you? Are you upset with my answer, or with all these hurry-walk-down-the-aisle stuff from my parents? Come on, we've been through this already."

He just couldn't get it. Rachel said, "I'm not angry with you, or with your dad and mum. I can understand their anxiety in wanting us to marry soon. But look, who's the angry chap here? Don't you feel angry with me when you have to say those words to your dad that you don't mean? Do you really agree with me that we're still young and still have to develop our careers, and so marriage can wait? Do you think by parroting my thoughts in front of your dad, it makes me feel better? I don't feel better! Relief for your saving grace in front of your dad, yes. But not better. Fancy a girl who having already decided her life-long partner being consumed by guilt just for deciding on a minor postponement in settling down? It's not fair, Colin, and I can't imagine you caused me this pain, yet you are the man I love. It's really not fair."

Angered by Rachel's sudden outburst, Colin wanted to react in kind. But he held his tongue. Rachel gradually composed herself, her voice softening. "Dear, yes, we've been here many times, but each time we are caught at the same point. Or rather, we always missed the whole point. I do not want to hurt you by delaying marriage. I know you're that trustworthy, committed family man who I want to spend my life with. I love children. But surely realising this dream a few years from now wouldn't hurt anything, would it?"

Silence lingered once more. The atmosphere was less tense. Colin felt she was also expecting him to say something – but what? He did not know what the 'right' words were. *Yes, that is very true, I should have been more understanding much earlier.* Or: *I did not parrot your thoughts in front of my dad to make me look understanding. I did that to save your face!* The difficult part, he bitterly realised, was that he felt Rachel was being unreasonable rather than seeking conciliation. So was he going to express his real feelings, an action he suspected he would regret later on?

HIDDEN DISABILITY

"**A**re you joking? How confident are you of handling university life?" Mrs Chua spoke and used sign language at the same time. Simultaneous Communication, as this signing mode is known.

I'm not joking! I've done a lot of serious thinking since the results came out last week. Getting a degree in Engineering could be my only big break in life! I'll give it a try no matter what. Joanne replied in sign language. Although Joanne had been taught in school to speak audibly, she had also been encouraged to practise her signing at home.

Mrs Chua could see how agitated her daughter was. But she was still doubtful. "You're not going to be able to catch up with the lectures. You were lucky to pass your A levels, even though your results were quite good. But you surely won't be able to manage in university without some form of special assistance."

Because I'm deaf.

It was a statement rather than a question.

"Right. Besides, you had such bad experiences in JC. Save for a few friends who don't mind associating with you, the rest of your classmates shunned you. Are you going to bank on immature university mates, cooped up in their ivory towers, to help you through your course? Forget it. You may have better luck in the working world."

But Ms Khoo thinks otherwise. She told me that some of the students in NTU have big hearts and sympathy for the deaf. They are generally very accommodating towards their deaf friends. Some of them even took it upon themselves to pick up sign language. Besides, I can hear. Joanne was signing rapidly.

"Ah," Mrs Chua raised an eyebrow. "So you discussed this with Ms Khoo and she supports your decision?" Rachel was about the only person Joanne's mum truly respected. There was no doubt in Mrs Chua's mind that the young lady's help was how her daughter even had the chance to enter university.

Right! Initially, I thought likewise and was not keen to relive my terrible experiences in school. I told her I preferred to find a job. She shared her experience of university life and how RSP (HI) has helped created a high level of deaf awareness and of other disabilities among the undergraduates.

The acronym RSP (HI) rang a bell with Mrs Chua – she vaguely remembered it from her interaction with the Deaf Association. This student group, which focused on helping the deaf community, ran tuition programmes for deaf children and other projects. One of these was a Chinese language course designed to acquaint deaf clients and their families with basic Chinese words, and Mrs Chua herself had previously signed up for it. She had not told her daughter she had enjoyed the course thoroughly. She started to waver. Since a club like RSP (HI) exists, perhaps the situation might not be that bad?

... also told me I'm not the first deaf undergraduate. There were several before me who had succeeded. I have always wanted to go to university because I know I have the ability to. Now I have the chance, how can I turn it down? Why should I? Joanne was increasingly animated. *Just because I might encounter lousy classmates?*

Mrs Chua glazed at her daughter intently. After eighteen years, she knew all too well Joanne's determination and temperance – strong as steel and fiery as a furnace. These traits were exactly the ones needed to succeed in an unforgiving world, made even harsher by her daughter's profound deafness. There and then, she made up her mind. "Yes. You're entitled to choose to pursue your dream. Go for it. I will support you."

For the first time since she received her A level results, Joanne smiled.

The Singapore Association for the Deaf (SADeaf) owed its humble beginnings in 1955 to Mr Peng Tsu Ying and his wife, both deaf, who had brought Shanghainese Sign Language to Singapore. The Association's mission was to improve the quality of life for people with hearing loss and also to prepare them to be integrated into society. In 1975, the Association set up the Vocational School for the Handicapped (now renamed Mountbatten Vocational School) which supplied hundreds of trained technicians to meet the young nation's need during that particular stage of its economic development. SADeaf also employed trained teachers to teach at the Singapore School for the Deaf (SSD), itself the result of a merger between Mr

Peng's Chinese Sign School for the Deaf and Oral School for the Deaf in 1963. SSD took in deaf students at the primary level and prepared them for continuing education in mainstream secondary schools. The Association today provides a wide range of services that includes hearing care service, support for deaf and hard-of-hearing students in mainstream schools, financial assistance for needy clients, accessibility services such as note-taking and sign language interpretation, as well as sign language courses and research.

Indeed, SADeaf has seen many changes through the decades; in fact, the only unchanged element in the Association would be its location. Its compound at Mountbatten Road was a blend of quaint 1960s design and modern amenities. The main building was a double-storey rectangular structure, with one of the longer sides extended like a tipped over 'P'. This section housed classrooms, meeting rooms, a computer lab, a dance studio for its performing groups and a cosy volunteer lounge. In front of these rooms within the rectangle was a small multi-purpose courtyard. To the west stood a low wall – 30 feet long by 5 feet tall – upon which was a painted mosaic. Just in front of the appendage to the rectangle was a dilapidated canteen with only one food stall, and benches and tables often used for volunteer discussions. The canteen was also the only part of SADeaf leading to Mountbatten Vocational School (MVS), via a short covered walkway, which occupied another half an acre of land.

Almost as varied as the functions of the Association was its people: deaf and hearing, staff, clients, public and volunteers, students and alumni. During the 2000s, this was especially so during the weekends when people from all walks of lives congregated and mingled as a single representation of deaf community. For many of them, coming here on a Saturday afternoon was a weekly routine. There were activities and conversations galore, but human voices were scant; most people were using sign language to converse.

Hey, Joanne, how? Huifen signed in a mixture of American Sign Language, Signing Exact English (SEE) signs and local signs – known as Singapore Sign Language (SgSL).

Huifen was a SSD teacher who was against teaching SEE to her deaf students. From her perspective, it might be a fact SEE helped deaf children to better grasp the English language and consequently in academic learning, but she found SEE too slow, too rigid and too dull. After all, sign language is a visual language and not suited to the syntax of most spoken languages (which SEE is modelled after). Besides, it has its own grammar and structure incorporating physical space and movement.

My mum agrees. Joanne signed word for word. Unlike Huifen, Joanne was a staunch SEE user. *I persuaded her to drop her objection to my plan to enrol in university.* Both she and I knew of the colossal hurdles (she finger-spelled 'colossal' as it was not in SEE's 5000-word signed vocabulary), *but I told her I will persevere no matter how difficult it gets.*

Huifen knew Joanne had the necessary determination and tenacity, and asked which course she had opted for.

Electrical and Electronics Engineering. NTU. I will submit my application form next week.

Good luck. I happy for you.

Thanks, it always feels better to have made a decision, for better or worse. Come to think of it, I've been too engrossed in deciding about this since my results came out that I haven't really bothered about other things around me...

Like your family? Huifen laughed.

Nay. My mum's fine. She has been with me on this issue. Glad to say she's been the only one lending me much-needed emotional support, other than Rachel of course. My dad is pretty much as usual. It probably worries me more to know he's taking an interest in my affairs. My brother, well, I suppose he is doing fine in there.

Henry Chua, Joanne's father, was not an intimate friend of Huifen's, but all the teachers at SSD knew the former school watchman as the passionate and caring Uncle Henry who often did double duty as the school's unofficial counsellor for students in distress of all kinds. That Joanne had often spoken in such a lukewarm way of him – it was bad enough not to hear praises of a man like Uncle Henry – of such a warm-hearted and lovely man reflected the bitter relationship between father and daughter.

Maybe he not talk to you, but he discuss with your mum this topic I sure, maybe form part of Mrs Chua's decision also. Please don't blame your father. Huifen urged, shaking her head and mouthing 'blame' to emphasise her point. Joanne was reading her old friend and mentor's signs purely from contextual deduction. Like some deaf persons whose first language is English, Joanne was more comfortable using SEE than native forms of sign.

Maybe. Joanne signed resignedly. *Enough of myself. How're uncle and aunt doing?* She was referring to Huifen's parents. Joanne had meant this question as a courteous follow-up. But she regretted this slip of tongue instantly. Joanne knew about Huifen's much messier situation. During her first six months as a baby, Huifen was seemingly a 'normal' child. At her birth, she had passed the 'bottom-smacking test', meant to check the newborn showed normal reactions and had healthy lungs – that is, by crying loudly when smacked. She was also startled by loud sudden sounds and turned her head to familiar voices. It was only at eighteen months that her parents realised she still had not responded to her own name, nor to common words like 'bye' and 'no'.

This learning development delay worried her parents a little, but not enough for them to seek medical advice. Even so, the difficulties their little girl had during her first three years were not apparent and only manifested in subtle ways. "Huifen is a late bloomer," her father would say. Then, one fateful morning, the wind chime – hung on the ceiling – dropped while Huifen's mother was feeding her. The mother jumped at the loud crash, but the toddler remained undisturbed. Little Huifen didn't even twitch. Her mother finally brought her to an ENT (Ear, Nose, Throat) specialist. That was it. At just over four years old, Huifen was diagnosed with profound hearing loss. Huifen's father consulted an old friend who referred them to SADeaf's Early Intervention Programme (EIP). That friend was Henry Chua, Joanne's father.

The first three years of life is the most critical period for the child's development of speech and language, and which consequently affects social, emotional and academic development. The EIP centre had recommended that Huifen be fitted with hearing aids and undergo auditory training to maximise her residual hearing; this would enable her to learn to communicate verbally. But her parents were against the idea, primarily because of the costs which the family could not afford, and also because Henry convinced them to enrol Huifen at SSD instead as he felt it would suit her better.

It was Joanne's opinion that her father's advice was the biggest mistake he had ever made. *Imagine how different Huifen's life would be if she had taken up the Natural Auditory-Oral approach which would have helped her to hear and speak? How could you ever deprive a child's chance to grow up in a normal way?* Choosing that path had solved the financial problem, but created a bigger one in its wake. Huifen's parents were not English educated and did not know sign language, so it was a struggle for them to understand one another. *The poor girl had not had a proper conversation with her parents since she was born,* Joanne had told her mum. The family used gestures to communicate with Huifen, and that was not good enough for her to express her innermost emotions, or for them to articulate to her theirs. In effect, Huifen had lost and had been lost to her parents at a tender age; a part of her and of them had always been mutually inaccessible.

They fine, Huifen gestured in reply, signing rapidly. Joanne suspected she was trying to mask her anguish. *We seldom talk each other, except small greetings, yes. Good health they, and I happy already.* A pause. *What else could I ask for?* The last sentence was deliberately signed very slowly. Her friend was right. Parents like hers were already a rare breed and she felt infinitely grateful that she had avoided the suffocating isolation suffered by many hard-of-hearing adults. What else could they ask for? Joanne didn't know.

Some visitors to the Association happened to walk past them and stopped to gawk at Joanne and Huifen's dialogue in sign language. This was a common reaction from hearing people, and the deaf had learned to ignore such stares. Suddenly Joanne quipped, *I wonder who's the real deaf here, us or them?*

Huifen glanced at the visitors, who had no idea they were being teased, and sniggered.

Yes, yes.

BEFRIENDERS

Daniel stood silent and grim as the stocky watchman in charge of his ward unlocked the steel gate leading to the stairways to Level Two. He and some roommates had been told two weeks ago that they were shortlisted for the new Boys Befrienders Programme. Every Thursday, the selected boys would attend a two-hour session with a group of undergraduate volunteers. Mrs Malathi, Head of Block E, had briefed Daniel, Peter, Wee Kiang and two other boys from the ward next door about the programme. Wee Kiang, known as 'The Scholar', was encouraged to use these sessions for tuition lessons as he would be sitting for a private examination in October. The other two boys, whom Daniel didn't know, were smiling away. Peter, from his own ward, was cooler; he simply let out a whistle and tried to look nonchalant. But there was a twinkle in his eyes; it seemed he, too, welcomed this new development.

"…I know you are all very happy to have the chance for these weekly meet-ups with the NTU volunteers. I hope you can make some friends from outside the Home, these young adults who wish to share their life experiences and give different perspectives." The boys were indeed delighted, but not for the reasons Mrs Malathi cited. Instead, it was the prospect of experiencing something new, of a change from the tedium of their daily routine.

"Before you leave, let me remind you that we selected you for this programme because of your good record and exemplary conduct. I wish to see you get the most out of these sessions," Mrs Malathi said. "But let me warn you too – if anyone tries any monkey business, I will call off the whole programme. Do you understand?"

On the day itself, Daniel found himself not liking the way the activity was conducted. It made him feel like being in a maximum security prison at Changi. (Not that Daniel had ever stepped into Changi Prison, but he had watched enough Hollywood films like *The Rock* and *The Green Mile* to think he knew exactly what it was like to be inside.) It always happened this way. At half past seven, the 'Privileged Three' were called upon by the watchman to get ready. Daniel, Peter and Wee Kiang held onto their textbooks. The rules forbade the boys to keep anything under their clothes. The thin and translucent robes they wore prevented that anyway. The watchman conducted a cursory visual inspection of their belongings before opening the door.

Once they stepped out to the hallway, he slammed shut the heavy doors which he then locked. The trio was then marched to the other end of the floor. The warden collected the two boys from the other ward in the same impassive way, and then led them to the infamous Wailing Gate. There, he halted, fished out a clanging bunch of keys attached to a big metallic ring from his right breast pocket, found the correct key, inserted it in the keyhole and twisted. Click. A creaky moan as the first gate swung open, revealing another keyhole on the inner gate. The watchman drew out another key to open it. Click. Then the inner gate swung open with an even more hideous wail. Daniel and his four companions – and all others who were watching from their wards – never became comfortable with this routine, despite having experienced it countless times. Somehow, the screeching of the gates seem to unearth, in an audible way, the sense of isolation and helplessness they had buried deeply within themselves, reminding them of their lost freedom.

Under watchful eyes, they shuffled in orderly fashion through the gates and down the two flights of stairs to Level Two. At the base of the stairs was a teak door painted blue. Next to the door was a card reader. The watchman tapped his security pass against the reader, waited a second, then pushed the door open. They came to another long corridor, quickened their pace and arrived at Activity Room One. The procession was over. In ten long minutes, the boys had marched through four locked doors. A guard then led the boys inside the room and now stood ten metres away. Daniel wondered if going up each of the eighteen levels of Hell would have been easier.

In Victor's mind, the procession conjured for him not images of transiting between Hell's eighteen halls, but something quite different. *Come on, even a simple passage from room to room had to be so heavily guarded!* When the Home staff brought Victor to Activity Room 1 at Level Two of the quadrangle building called Block E, he had first caught sight of the tall, burly warden (sent to fetch the other boys) at the door of a ward upstairs that spanned half the length of the squarish block. He saw three boys emerge from the ward, following their warden along the corridor to another identical ward at the adjacent side of the floor, where two more boys joined the line. They had then proceeded to the northeast corner of the quadrangle building with a pair of heavy gates just before the stairways – Victor surmised it was a fortified structure designed to contain any incidents of coordinated rioting from the sleeping quarters.

From where Victor was, he could make out another pair of gates at the southwest corner of Level Three as well. He craned his head to look at Level Four. It too had heavy steel gates barring the stairways at two diagonally opposite corners, positioned southeast and northwest. About the same time, the five boys at Level Three were walking in a single file – they were keeping perfect pace – down to their rendezvous with Victor and his fellow volunteers, another warden was bringing a different group of boys on the fourth floor in the opposite direction to the northwest gate, before disappearing into the stairways. These were well-considered riot control manoeuvres to segregate the residents, while they were on the move, to minimise the risk of any misconduct, Victor thought. *What evil had these boys committed to result in such harsh measures being foisted upon them?* The corollary was even more dismaying: *How would it affect them psychologically?*

The boys finally reached the room. Each of the volunteers had been paired up with a boy as his befriender. The volunteers had also been shown the boys' photos for easy identification. Victor was assigned to a Daniel Lok Kai Mun, 14, an affable-looking chap who had committed theft. In person, Daniel was quite tall.

"Hello, my name's Victor."

"Daniel." They shook hands.

All around the room, the NTU student befrienders were introducing themselves to the younger boys, who were apparently too overwhelmed to react appropriately. *Hi, I'm Peter… I'm Tom…Call me Wee Kiang...* The introductions were terse; both groups knew they would have time to understand each other better.

"Excuse me, boys. May I have your attention please? I'm Susan, the coordinator for this session." Susan was a petite girl with a cheerful smile. "Boys, we're volunteers from Welfare Services Club in NTU. This is the third year we're having this project with you guys. We, and the Home, have meant for this project as a regular interaction session between you and our students. We're here to be friends and elder brothers and sisters, and to learn from each other. I'm sure you have as much to share with us as we have to share with you..."

"Can I share your bed?" One boy piped up. The others broke into wild guffaws. Susan was unflustered. Still smiling, she simply said, "No, my friend, you can't." This made them stop laughing.

"Do you share your bed with your elder sister at home too?" Susan's tone was now slightly admonishing. The culprit kept silent and frowned. *Cool lady*, Daniel thought, *defusing the insulting joke like that.*

Susan moved on. "Alright, now meet your new friend in front of you. You'll have the next hour to know how friendly they all are. Volunteers, enjoy your chat!" The pairs dispersed to the neatly arranged chairs scattered across the room.

Victor and Daniel found a spot away from the others. "So, tell me more about yourself," Victor prompted.

"I'm Daniel." That was all.

His curt response did not surprise Victor. He thought, *Daniel is probably just like me, a man of few words. Well, anyone would be when asked to talk about himself by someone he had known for only five minutes.* He decided to change his approach.

"Oh? You don't look like your age, Daniel. You look more mature. My elder brother, Peter, looks even younger than you. And he's almost thirty."

Daniel shrugged. Victor tried again, "I'd like to know more about your life here. Maybe you can share with me what you do here, who's your best chum in your block, anything you want to talk about."

Daniel thawed a little at the mention of Victor's brother. It reminded him of his own brother Peter, which also happened to be the name of his bunkmate. Such a coincidence!

Then, suddenly, a torrent: "What can I possibly do in this shithole? All of us start our day at six-thirty every morning, do some useless PT till seven before we are given breakfast. After that, it is either Technical or Maths or English taught to us which don't really do us any good. Not when the teachers are more disciplinarians than educators. And they're not qualified teachers anyhow. Then there is the dog watch at four pm, where we do some ball games at the court. Dinner's at six, and some TV after that, but all the programmes are either evening news or documentaries, all boring stuff which no one likes…"

Victor was nodding as Daniel rattled on. He was trying hard to suppress a smile. All kids are like that. When it came to complaining about about life, they could be grouchier than an eighty-year-old lady.

"… then they herd us all back to our dorms, lights off at ten."

Then Daniel became silent. Victor waited a while more. Still nothing.

"Right. That sounds pretty much like what I went through during my days in OCS. You know, Officer Cadet School." *That was just nine months. This boy has been here trice as long. No wonder he looked more like a veteran soldier than a school kid.* "Life's tough, I agree. But what don't kill us often makes us stronger."

Daniel remained silent.

Victor tried to explain. "Okay, what I mean is, look at the bright side of life. Things here are tough, but they also toughen you up. So when you get out of here, it'll be easy for you, not harder. Don't you agree?"

Bullshit! How would you know what life here is like, and if it would do me good or harm next time? But Daniel decided to be polite. "How do you know it'd do me good when I'm out? You barely know what it's like here."

"That's true, but from the programme you described to me, I think the Home has a good plan to prepare you for life after you are released. See, you do vocational training, academics and sports here. Those make for a balanced regime, catering to everyone's different aptitudes and interests, I suppose. You sit for private examinations in here so you won't waste your time and lose out to your contemporaries out there, or at least, not too much." Victor regretted using the words 'in' and 'out', worrying it evoked negative thoughts in Daniel. "And the discipline the Home imposed, you know, is probably going to serve you well in life later on. That's something some other teenage boys do not get and they suffer when they enrol in NS."

Right. They don't get dirty sneakers stuffed into their mouths by bullies, or locked up in confinement rooms for days for being defiant to their teachers. Daniel was tuning out of the conversation with his befriender, who seemed to be either emphasising the kindness of the Home or preaching about the goodness of life after this. *How patronising and unsympathetic!* He wanted to opt out of this programme. But somehow, strangely, a nagging voice in his mind was urging him to think again. Victor might appear patronising and off-putting, but there was something different about him.

"So what plans do you have for the rest of today?" Daniel decided to change the topic. "Just talk?"

"Yes. I'm your friend right? So we'll have to talk more to each other to understand each other better."

Daniel had never realised in all his fourteen years that you could befriend somebody simply because the other party wanted to, and you did that by cooping up in a room with him, two hours a week, and talking non-stop. *This was ridiculous. Was this one of those idiotic adult ideas again? Surely my own personal views about that person counted in making friends. So why didn't Victor, or anyone else, consult me, or asked me if we could be friends, instead of making assumptions?*

Daniel stared at him. "How old are you?"

"I'm twenty-six, twenty-five and ten months to be exact. My birthday falls in December," Victor replied. Perhaps volunteering information implied sincerity and helped get your partner to open up to you. "Why do you ask?"

Daniel said, "Because I've never heard of friends with such a wide age gap. Uncles yes, cousins, maybe." *And you're too fake for my liking.* He did not say it out loud.

"Ah, you heard of the saying friendship transcends all races and ages?" He explained, "It means that no matter how our ages differ, that is no reason to stop us from being friends. Or you may consider me as your elder brother or cousin, but not uncle please."

Daniel saw the crack and immediately exploited it with glee, "Okay, then you'll be Uncle Victor to me. How's that?"

Ah, this kid is cheeky. Victor nodded. "Sure, if that makes you feel good. Now, Daniel, is there anything you'd like to know about me?"

"Do you have a younger sister? Tell me more about her. How many girlfriends do you have?"

God, kids are always kids, Victor thought, *wherever they are. They'd jump at any opportunity to ask exactly the awkward questions you didn't want to answer.*

"No and no," he replied dryly.

FIRST JOB

Colin Lee stared at the washroom mirror as he shaved. He seemed to have aged visibly. When did that happen? he wondered. He quickly dismissed the thought and finished washing up – he had an appointment with Tim Soon's parents.

Colin had always regarded his determination and ability to focus as his key asset. Once he set his mind to do something, he would almost always complete it. This trait had propelled Colin through his education – from being a laggard in primary school to second place in his junior college batch, and then topping his Electronics and Electrical Engineering cohort of 1,200 at NTU. He had, quite aptly, been christened 'Small Ant' by his secondary school classmates, due to his small frame which seemed inexhaustible. Some years later, a friend described him as "nuclear-powered, determined to burn up every ounce of fuel in his reserves in his pursuit for excellence". Colin's ego did swell slightly from such praise, but he thought the nuclear fission analogy was more appropriate to describe one of his other attributes – the more energy you stored initially, the more explosive it became subsequently. Simply put, initial success and achievement did not, and could not, distract him from his many plans in life. Academic excellence was just one of them.

He quickly changed out of his pyjamas into a polo tee and a pair of Adidas sneakers and went out. It was eight-thirty and the Foos' place was only fifteen minutes' brisk walk away. Saturday morning pedestrian traffic, however, was light. Colin took his time to walk over. Moments like this – being able to indulge in contemplative thought – were what fuelled his hyper-focus nature and boosted his efficiency. But he had to admit he could overdo it at times, such as reading a book as he crossed the road, or even practising signing a song from the radio as he drove! Rachel had ticked him off about this many times, to no avail.

Colin was a devotee of multi-tasking due to his belief in effective time management as the way to a rich and purposeful life. Boredom was his nemesis; he disliked purely mundane tasks like having a meal or a long train ride. Besides, he felt multi-tasking wasn't at all difficult as long as you know how to do it well. *You divided your mind into two functionary units: the smaller bit to execute the boring mundane task and leaving the bulk of your mental functions to take on the more challenging task.* Which was what he was doing – using his sight and sense of direction to navigate the streets of Jurong while his mind was miles away.

Mr and Mrs Foo had never been able to come fully to terms with Tim Soon's disability. They had also not forgiven themselves for the delay in seeking medical treatment when Tim Soon was struck by dengue fever eighteen years ago. What had gone some way to heal their grieving hearts was their sense of fatalism – they believed Fate had played a bad joke on them, that certain things were meant to be and not under their control. It also helped that Tim Soon, with an IQ of 52, had mild to moderate intellectual disability. He was able to grasp simple concepts and be taught simple tasks. Some of them, such as folding clothes, he even performed with more satisfactory results than a non-disabled child might accomplish. At age six, his speech had developed to the point where it was indistinguishable from anyone else's. At eight, Tim Soon was referred to the Movement for the Intellectually Disabled Singapore (MINDS), where he underwent a series of tests to assess his cognitive, communication and motor skills. He was classified as being 'mid-to-high level functioning' and was enrolled into Jurong Gardens School, a special education institution for students with intellectual disability.

Technically, with his IQ score, Tim Soon should have qualified to enrol into a special school, which was the closest a child with intellectual disability could come to receiving a primary education, and from there, could even aim to enter the mainstream route to a vocational certificate and even open employment. However, his intellectual grading of 'moderate-to-mild' just missed the special schools' admission criteria by a wispy margin. The less mentally rigorous educational approach at Jurong Gardens School might, comparatively, stymie Tim Foo's mental growth and diminish his future potential. Yet, the thought of appealing against this assignation did not occur to Mr and Mrs Foo. They took this arrangement to be another of Heaven's plans and followed along. For the couple, admission to a school was already a bonus – they had not expected their child to be granted an education since that fateful dengue fever incident. Why should it matter what kind of school he went to?

Tim Soon's school days were happy ones. At Jurong Gardens School, his lessons included ADL (Activities of Daily Living), basic arithmetic and English, as well as sports and games. But beyond his family and school environments, he had no other exposure to the larger social realm. Yet Tim Soon was far from lonely; in the day, he always looked forward to school and meeting his good friends. After school, he would long for his family's attention. Tim Soon was also a mild-tempered and well-mannered child, lacking the common issues of resentment or anger that most kids experienced.

Mr Foo, the sole family breadwinner, worked as a bus driver for an upscale transport company which served high-end hotels. It was a job from which he derived much satisfaction and pride, and he was also fairly compensated. Job insecurity was not a concern to Mr Foo either, as his company valued experienced staff. And while, at fifty, he was no longer at his physical peak, the fitness requirement of a driver wasn't all too daunting.

He could still make ends meet.

"Now, Uncle, Tim Soon has been accepted into the Employment Development Centre, EDC in short. He can start work at the Margaret Drive Centre next week." Mr and Mrs Foo were seated opposite Colin as he delivered the good news. Tim Soon was not around. Colin badly wanted to tell Tim Soon at once, but first he needed to discuss something with the parents in private.

"Oh, thank you, Colin. That's really fast. We only sent in the application to MINDS two weeks ago. They are really efficient, aren't they?"

"Well, the social worker is," Colin said. "After all, Tim Soon's a bright boy. The school principal has been full of praises for him all along. I guess he must have written in to EDC recommending Tim Soon for the programme."

"That silly boy's not bright. He owes a lot to the teachers at Jurong Gardens, and the principal of course." Both of them leant towards Colin in gratitude. "And you in particular. Thank you for all you have done for Tim Soon."

"Think nothing of it, Uncle. It's my pleasure. Besides, I've learnt a lot from Tim Soon too. There were times when I was inspired by him, especially his strong character that wouldn't budge under pressure." Colin said. "And he certainly is wiser than most people think!"

"Yes, you are right. I may have better luck trying to get Tim Mei to take a puff of the cigarette than convincing Tim Soon to try." Mr Foo laughed. He was in a good mood, so Colin seized the chance.

"Uncle and auntie, actually there's something I wish to discuss with you."

This time, it was Mrs Foo who broke into a smile. "Of course, please feel free to speak your mind." She must had detected Colin's hesitation and knew something was brewing.

"I'm sure both of you are very happy with Tim Soon's acceptance into the EDC programme. But then, two months back, straight after his graduation from Jurong Gardens School, I had another thought. Surely Tim Soon is capable enough to do more than pack used headsets into bags or make handicrafts for sale. He has the potential to do much more. Even so, I know Tim Soon would enjoy working at EDC, just as he had had a good time at JGS. You see? He does not aspire to be more, but he definitely has the potential to be. Why don't we do something for him to achieve that?"

"What can we do?" Mr Foo interrupted. He was taken aback. "Isn't EDC the right place for him to take the next step towards independence?"

"Uncle, I was thinking of something else. Open employment. A totally unsheltered environment for Tim Soon that will accelerate his growing process. And I think he's ready to step out, to join society. Even before you requested me to apply for his enrolment into EDC, I'd already sent out several letters to some employers to ask if they would consider Tim Soon for a job. One of them, a grocer, asked if Tim Soon can count and do simple accounting, to which I replied no to the latter, but explained he could be trained. He was kind enough to reply he'd consider if Tim Soon's trained. Another, a confectionery, said they needed no more hands at the shop front but needed help in the kitchen. The only problem was the hot and stifling environment, and he asked if Tim Soon could stand it. I was unsure either, so I took the liberty to decline the offer."

Mr Foo said, "Of course you should decline it. We really have no wish to put our son through such hardship, just to qualify for some accelerated life-learning course. He has a hard enough life already. I also understand your good intentions for Tim Soon, Colin. At first, I wondered how you find these employers. Then I remembered you mentioned before your mum has worked at the neighbourhood market for many years. Your commitment really touches us, but since Tim Soon has already secured a place at EDC, let this open employment hunt just rest here, shall we?"

Colin tried again. "Uncle, I'm not trying to push Tim Soon into the deep end of the pool just to teach him to swim independently. But I'm saying that we should not just be contented with him staying in the wading pool, as he grows taller. And Tim Soon *is* taller than many others among his peers. The JGS teachers said so, the principal said so, and the volunteers of RSP (ID) said so. We all believe he has what it takes to be learning to swim at the deeper end. Look at the merits of open employment: he develops a sense of self-worth and self-confidence, improves his integration into the outside world, becomes more independent, and can also earn more than at EDC."

At this, Mr Foo retorted, "I've a good-paying job. We don't need him to earn a bigger paycheck! And to be frank, we have come to terms with his disability that we no longer wish fervently that he would get much better. My wife and I are happy to fulfil our roles as his parents, as what Heaven must have arranged when they sent us this son, as parents who will protect him and provide for him for as long as we can. We're happy as long as he's happy."

And may I ask how on earth do you know he won't be happy working outside? But again, Colin knew better to keep this comeback to himself. At the end of the day, Colin respected Mr Foo's opinion, though he did not agree with it. "I understand, uncle. We all have Tim Soon's interest at heart. Since we agree he'll fit in well and happily in EDC, that's all which matters."

LOOKING BACK IN REMORSE

It was a cool and starless night. Victor was snug in bed and sleepless. His mind was in turmoil and memories of the distant past kept bubbling to the surface. Some memories were best left buried, Victor had realised a long time ago, and so he had tried his utmost to leave them be. But when Daniel, his assigned boy at SBH, had cheekily asked whether he has a sister, his resolve to detach himself, to remain stoic, instantly broke down.

The memories came rushing back.

It was 1995. Victor was at home studying when Mum and Wai Leng returned from an appointment with the neurologist at the National University Hospital (NUH). By then, Victor had grown apathetic to the results of his sister's medical reviews. Since the best doctors in Singapore could not pinpoint her illness after so many consultations, what was the point of asking? If they had discovered something new beyond the initial diagnosis of "protein strain deficiency in her mitochondria", he would get to know about it soon or later.

That day, he remembered how shocked he had been when Wai Leng suddenly stormed into the living room and turned on the radio at full blast. Mum was in the bathroom and Dad was reading the newspapers. Victor had stomped out of his room and told Wai Leng off. But she ignored him and continued to hum tunelessly to the blaring music. Angered, Victor slapped her upper arm. Whack! No effect. Victor then grabbed her arms and shook her violently. "You idiot! Turn down the radio!"

Wai Leng finally reacted – tears streamed down her pale cheeks and she started to yell incoherently, not from pain but from some inner, unarticulated anguish. Victor could feel his own tears welling too, but he had lost control of himself and continued to shake and pummel Wai Leng. Wai Leng crumbled to the floor and kept yelling. Dad was also shouting. Mum ran out of the bathroom and attempted to pull Victor away. It was utter chaos. But everyone froze when Mum started crying too. Things settled down somewhat. Wai Leng, still on the floor, was whimpering. Victor returned to his room, in tears. Peter, who had came out of his room during the fracas, and Mum simply stood where they were, as in a daze. Dad started for the door and went out, slamming the door.

Startled, Victor touched his face. His cheeks were damp. Had he been crying? How vivid that scene remained, after nine long years! Unbidden, another memory arose.

1996. Wai Leng's frail body had seemed to shrink even more, ravaged by the high dosages of the medicine and drugs she had to take. It had also affected her cognitive ability. She could no longer keep up in class. Doctors advised her rest at home, for good. This certainly was not a good sign.

That morning, Wai Leng was helping Mum to peel some onions in the kitchen. Victor was studying in his room.

Thump!

Victor ran out to see Wai Leng lying on her back on the floor. She was convulsing – her third epilepsy attack in the previous six months. It was as if her bony limbs were strung to some powerful invisible forces jerking upon them. With practised efficiency, Mum pushed her body to a side position and tapped her face lightly to make sure she remained conscious, while Victor checked her airway was open and her tongue was in the normal resting position to facilitate drainage of accumulated saliva. Wai Leng's jaws were clamped tight. Nobody called for the ambulance either; from past experience, it was unnecessary. Epilepsy attacks came and went in brief spasms. Once, they had taken her to the hospital's A&E, but she had merely been placed on a drip and her attending neurologist had been nonchalant: "She's going to be fine."

Mum and Victor held on to Wai Leng's shuddering limbs to avoid any unintentional injuries inflicted onto herself. This part was easy. What strength were they expecting in a body long tormented by this condition? Victor stared at his sister's pallid face. Wai Leng's eyes were open wide but void of expression and emotion. Hers was a face Victor had known since childhood, but at that moment, she seemed to be a stranger. He had seen photos of her in kindergarten – so adorable, bright and plump. (Mum always said that of her three children, Wai Leng was the most chubby baby.)

How could a benevolent God have allowed this? Victor was in despair. He was also guilt-ridden. He loved Wai Leng; they were very close. In fact, the mere two-year age gap between them was why she was closer to him than his older brother, Peter, was. Yet he had hit her when his frustration got the better of him. He had even suggested sending her away, on the grounds that only Tampines Home had the expertise to care for her.

The wall clock chimed and Victor was jolted back to the present again. How long had he been being lost in the past? He didn't know. This family history was something he had hidden from everyone – he had not breathed a word even to his closest friends. How far was he prepared to reveal this shrouded past to Daniel, assuming he asked again?

His mind slipped further back and the years fell away. Victor revisited other fragments of memories, an endless stream of them. He recalled how he hated coming back to this home after school, how he had chosen to immerse himself completely in studies as an emotional anaesthesia, and how, even if he were at home, he utterly ignored his sister. He thought about his self-sacrificing mother, who had borne the brunt of the physical and emotional burden of being Wai Leng's caregiver. She had given Wai Leng dedicated care and was her psychological anchor, to the extent her own body and spirit had suffered greatly. Mother and daughter, through the years, had developed a bond and closeness that transcended kinship; they were dancing a waltz of life in tandem; they had gone through the darkest hours together.

So, in Mum's heart, Wai Leng had never really left. For years after, she recalled and recounted stories about Wai Leng to the others, refusing to let her memory fade. She lamented how ill-fated she was in losing her only daughter, and how other parents had daughters to care for them in old age. To her, daughters would always be different from sons. Despite so, she continued to extend her selfless gift to her two sons after Wai Leng's departure. *Maybe she wasn't the best mother in the world,* Victor used to tell himself, *but she had to be the mother most deserving of compassion and piety.*

He thought of the scene near the end, when they were around her hospital bed for the final time. They had been too late. Mum had collapsed wailing, while he and Peter ran out of the ward and cried. Though Victor thought he would be mentally prepared and would not be too sad – he told himself it was better for her to go than endure prolonged suffering – the reality proved him wrong.

Victor also made a promise that day. *My dear sister, rest assured I'll take good care of Mum forever. That must be your last wish and it is my only way to make it up to you.* Dad didn't shed a single tear though. This tore at Victor. *How could he could be so callous and unfeeling? I hate him.*

The following Thursday evening, the RSP volunteers gathered at NTU and took a short bus ride to the Singapore Boys' Home (SBH). Outside the gate, they showed their identity cards to the guards before filing through a turnstile into the compound. At the visitor holding area, a pre-session briefing was conducted for them. They were rather rowdy, much to the displeasure of the Home's security detail.

At SBH, a classification and assessment tool was used to identify the inmates' needs and the risk factors objectively and accurately. Individual care plans were drawn up for each resident, and an inter-disciplinary team, which included psychologists and psychiatrists, conducted assessments and intervention. The classification and assessment system also helped determine the allocation of the residents to the three rehabilitative units – Blocks B, D and E. The most well-behaved boys were assigned to B while the worse ended up in E. The really good ones went into the Singapore Boys' Hostel, which was really closer to being a boarding school than a reformative institution.

Most of the NTU RSP (Youth) volunteers chose Block D, which was regarded as the easiest assignment. The few Block E volunteers, among them Victor, did not see their choice as an act of bravado. Just a plain, logical one. To them, it was simply because when you wanted to join RSP (Youth), you wanted to know not just another spoilt brat or school bully, but a real hardcore case. They were the ones who could really impart life lessons from a fresh and unique perspective. Whether they were converted into angels or remained unmoved by your weekly preaching at the end of the day did not matter. That was the whole point, as he saw it.

But right then, they had a problem. This was only their third session and half his fellow volunteers were losing steam. Trying to break through the stone walls their boys had put up was like hitting their heads against it. The others were not doing much better. It had dawned on them that talking with their boys in one-to-one sessions was the easiest way to bore everyone involved, till one side gave up. In view of the somewhat desperate situation, Susan, the block coordinator, suggested holding group conversations to spice up the dialogue sessions.

"Why don't we pair up a senior with a junior and their boys? Double team. I'm sure they'll feel less intimidated when they have friends by their side," Shafid ventured. He knew that the freshmen, more so than the boys, felt less intimidated if they were paired up. A third-year Mechanical Engineering student, Shafid had a lot of street cred with the boys. His assertiveness and boldness had earned him their respect, and his ability to converse in Hokkien was definitely another reason for his popularity (he had picked up enough elementary Hokkien from the boys to pass as a Chinese over the phone). He was also diplomatic and able to defuse explosive situations that inevitably came up.

"Shafid and Susan are right," another volunteer said, "We ought to try something different. My boy's been giving me the cold shoulder since the first session. We have nothing to talk about. He's the quiet kind who gives one-word answers to all my questions. Throughout the session, he was reading the *Cleo* magazine I bought for him. When I asked about his favourite singers, he just shook his head. When I saw boys like Wee Kiang so engrossed chatting with Susan, I can't help but feel demoralised."

"You misunderstood," Susan clarified. "Wee Kiang was only trying to fish Wenxin's phone number from me." Wenxin, with anime-like eyes and a petite figure, was the prettiest volunteer.

"Yes, there will be some difficulties in the beginning, which is why Susan suggested the pairing up system. I'm sure things will improve," Shafid tried to reassure them. "About bringing in reading materials for the boys, I don't think it's helpful. Doesn't help in understanding your boys at a deep level, especially in the beginning. You need to engage them in more personal ways – listen to them, open up to them, relate to them. Maybe try fun activities within your little groups of four, such as solving puzzles or word quizzes. These boys are smarter than we think."

He paused. Most of the volunteers nodded.

Susan chipped in, "Yes, we understand your apprehension. I am looking at organising a volunteer workshop with the professional counsellors at the ministry next month. Hopefully, they can give us some insights on how to engage the boys more effectively. Ok, now, are we ready for this evening's session?" There was no answer, but everyone seemed more cheerful, which was some consolation.

"Good! Alright, Emily will pair up with Jane, Wenxin with Justri. Shafid with Lisa, Victor with me..."

Coalesce

"This country will not be a good place for any of us to live in unless we make it a good place for all of us to live in."

Theodore Roosevelt

CHOICES

Transcript from *I-Seek-You*, a webchat portal, between members 12418899 and 42563336. 282305, on 16 November 2004.

<RK>   Hi, Joanne!

<JC>   Hello, Ms Khoo.

<RK>   Call me Rachel. I'm not that old lah. :) How's your school vacation so far?

<JC>   Haha ok! Not good leh. Taking an inter-semester general elective which I have no interest in.

<RK>   I see. Well, at least you have the chance to clear your module during the vacation. Most of the time, these slots are allocated to the seniors.

<JC>   I know. But it's so boring. So language based. Afraid I'll not be able to pass. Besides, the exam results are out in two weeks' time. I worry I'll fail at least two modules.

<RK>   Come on. From experience, exam results usually turn out better than we expect. Moderation of grades always saves the day. Cheer up!

<JC>   You sure? Ok, actually I'm alright. You know what? Am getting the hang of life here. Been only one semester but I feel more settled than when I was in JC1. Surviving very well here. Well, I'm smart - I guess. <joking>

<RK>   Great to hear that! So how're your course mates? Nice? Or avoiding you like in JC?

<JC>   No, actually they were quite intrigued by me! I have made three good kakis here. All of them treat me normally. Phew! And that feels really good! They are really warm and helpful.

<RK>   Referring to your WSC friends? The people there are good, aren't they? And of course, RSP (HI). They must have started practising for their annual Christmas Signed Carolling event. Joining them?

<JC>   Mm. I'm not really into WSC events. No affinity to WSC. It's not really doing what it's supposed to do. Yah, there are those who genuinely want to help. But in general, when it comes to raising public awareness of the disabled, I don't think they've done enough. And nope, I'm not in the carolling.

<RK>   About raising public awareness, that's only one part of WSC's mission. It has organised camps, carnivals, plays and other special projects aimed at educating the public. Don't these show it's making the effort? Take the annual carolling event – it shows people the deaf can appreciate music too.

<JC>   Ok lah. Maybe you're right. I can agree WSC's done a fantastic job, but that's outside the school community. But what about internally? You know most of the professors here have never heard of WSC? My lecturers just rattled on and on during tutorials. A few tutors simply refused to repeat what they said when I couldn't catch them and I spoke up about it. Said they cannot slow the entire class down because of one student. Wahlau! Made my blood boil! I gave up, just copied as much notes as I could. One of my deaf friends studying in NUS told me she feels NUS is more conducive for deaf students.

<RK>   Oh dear! But I believe these are individual lecturers and tutors who are not so understanding or empathic. And not as if the university itself is that unfeeling. Surely there must be one or two professors who empathise with you?

<JC>   Oh yes. But they're rare leh. Like, two of my lecturers were fantastic. They always make sure I'm seated right next to them during tutorials so I can hear them better. After the class, they would check with me if I can keep up and revise with me if not. I am very grateful to them.

<RK>   Well, as I like to say, there're always good-hearted people everywhere. Compared to NTU, NUS might seem more accommodating because it is more established and has had more experience with undergraduates with disabilities. Some years back, a friend from NUS told me a student body set up a club to identify deaf peers on the campus and informed the lecturers so that the deaf students could get help. Like, provide tape recorders to allow them to replay the lecturers' lessons at home.

<JC>   Eh. That's overdoing things lah. We're not that helpless! We only need a little more consideration from the lecturers. Like, for those who tend to rattle away, they can speak slower. I don't think the deaf students want special attention or treatment. Makes them self conscious too.

<RK>   That's right. In fact, the club disbanded two years ago. Apparently, the deaf students ended up feeling too much pressure from the extra attention. But after that, I hope at least there was more awareness among staff of the deaf students' needs.

<JC>   Well, what to do. People tend to think that the deaf or those with other disabilities cannot do anything well. That's unfair loh. We're as capable as the non-disabled. Confirm. As long as suitable adaptations are in place to allow us full and equal access. Like, speaking clearly and facing us during communication. Are we asking for too much?

<RK>   No...

<JC>   So much for the public awareness WSC has been advocating. Some students I met deliberately exaggerate their lips movement when they speak. Sigh! As if all deaf people know how to lip read. They don't realise most of us can't! Besides, we can hear!

<RK>   Well, I feel you just have to educate them. Think about it – at least they bothered to make the effort to communicate, even if they didn't do so properly.

<JC>   What makes me even madder was that some of them made rude gestures with their hands and faces, and thought we would appreciate that.

\<RK\> I can imagine how pissed off you were. But rather than chewing them up, you can say politely: "Thanks for the miming, but I can hear you." Or perhaps they thought you use sign language.

\<JC\> But I'm from Canossian School, not SSD. How do they suppose I can go to an university if I can only sign but can't hear?

\<RK\> Ah now, SSD does offer Auditory-Verbal Therapy. The students there do learn speech too. Obviously most people you encounter don't know all these. I can sense the more friendly vibes from the students around you compared to your college days. They may be ignorant but at least they try and are making the first move. Try to be more open to them too, ok?

\<JC\> Yah. That's true. I will. Just venting lah.

\<RK\> I'm glad so. OK. All the best for your studies. It's late. Got to go. See you.

\<JC\> Night, Ms….Oops… Rachel. =)

———⌗———

At the same moment, Joanne's parents were mulling over much the same topic. At work, Henry Chua had suffered the bad luck of having a ladder fall on his thigh. Fortunately, it was a minor accident and he was not seriously injured. Mrs Chua was rubbing medical balm onto the bruise. It looked bad, having turned a shade of blue-black. They could hear, faintly, the sounds of typing from Joanne's mechanical keyboard.

"She's at it again. Straight into her room after dinner and online ever since. What's the time now? Almost ten!" Henry Chua was unhappy.

"Just let her be. Joanne's a sensible girl. She knows what she's doing. We never have to worry about her studies, right? So far, she hasn't complained about any troublemakers in school. She said NTU's fine. Her schoolmates are more mature and her lecturers more patient."

"How do you know for sure? She only said all that so you won't worry," Henry insisted. "She might have problems which she is keeping to herself."

Mrs Chua had anticipated her husband's disgruntlement, but that didn't made her any less annoyed. She stopped kneading and sat up straight. "You are one stubborn mule. How long more will it take before you see it? Joanne didn't go against you. She only wanted to choose how she lives her life. What would you have done in her shoes? Willing to give up a life of sounds and language at seven when deafness struck, then took up signing just so her father wanted her to? She has to live with her deafness for the rest of her life, not us. After all these years, you are still disapproving of her choice."

"What's wrong with Total Communication? So many deaf children were taught via that approach at SSD for so many years. Didn't Huifen do fine and go to Ngee Ann Polytechnic? Now she's a teacher. Who says SSD students using TC can't excel? Besides, the Natural Auditory-Oral approach practised by Canossian School isn't for us."

"But she had enough residual hearing so she didn't qualify for a cochlear implant." Mrs Chua pointed out. She was thinking of the scene more than ten years ago when Joanne, just seven years old then, was stricken by a viral infection that had diminished her hearing permanently, and how brave she had been through the ordeal. She was also determined to continue learning to develop her listening and speaking skills. Some Canossian School students with more severe hearing loss were offered cochlear implants. Also known as a CI, it was an electronic device which has to be implanted via an operation into the inner ear, and enable the implantee to hear and understand sounds better. For Joanne, this extremely expensive surgical operation was not an option; a hearing aid would do. Mrs Chua continued, "Besides, if not for Canossian, Joanne would never have made it to where she is today."

Henry was defeated and knew it. He had been deeply attached to the signing culture and community all his life and those were exactly the reasons for his belief in TC. When Henry allowed himself to be totally honest, he would concede Joanne's choice all those years ago was the right one. In fact, he had cheered privately when Joanne had taken her less-disciplined younger brother in hand, and was proud of Joanne's excellent PSLE results, even if he didn't show it. It was his ego which had got in the way; he refused to admit to his family that he had been wrong.

"And our poor son," Henry said softly. He had changed the subject. "Each time we visit him, he would say he's fine inside. But I can tell he bears a grudge against us. He thinks we neglected him because of Joanne. He didn't want to talk about her. I don't know. Whose fault is it actually?"

"You know he doesn't fully understand, old man. It's not Joanne's fault he landed in jail. It's probably our fault. Sigh! We were the ones who neglected him. We were the ones who devoted our attention to

Joanne so much that he didn't get enough guidance from us. It's all our fault, old man." Mrs Chua was tearful.

Henry cradled his head with his hands. "Poor boy. He was so bright and good natured. He did so well in school. Who would expect him to mix with bad company? That evening when he was caught, if Joanne hadn't flared up at him, called him names, he would not have left home and ended up doing all those stupid deeds."

"The boy was also in the wrong. Too wayward, too immature. Jealous? For what? His deaf sister who needed more attention? She was not wrong to scold him that evening, just a bit too harsh. She has been feeling very bad about it all these years. We were the most culpable."

"You're right. We caused their misery," Henry replied in resignation.

REACHING OUT

Life is a strange and unpredictable affair. Just as how two lumps of carbon buried deep within Earth's interior, by random forces of nature, could coalesce into diamond and coal, so could two parallel lives develop into dissimilar characters. Daniel and Colin's family backgrounds were similar enough as to give no inkling of the divergent paths the boys would grow up to take. Fate was equally unkind to them in different ways.

There were times when Colin disliked his family. He remembered, vaguely, how this dislike had been sparked off by one isolated incident on the eve of his secondary two examinations. For reasons he could no longer recall, his parents, out of the blue, erupted into a fierce quarrel and ended up in a physical altercation. It became a literal fight, with the short, stocky Mr Lee grabbing and shoving his scrawny wife. Alerted by the noise, Colin had ran out and grabbed his father, pushing and restraining him against the wall. Their eyes met for a long instant before Mr Lee calmed down and stopped struggling to free himself.

But by then, the traumatised Mrs Lee had already called the police to accuse her husband of domestic violence. The police arrived – the neighbours gawking at the sight of the men in blue – and issued a stern warning to Mr Lee after some questioning. After they left, the Lee family lapsed into silence for the rest of the night. Colin no longer had the mood to carry on studying and had an early night. He could not stop brooding over the incident that night and for a long time afterward – it had left an indelible scar on his psyche.

That turned out to be the first of a number of occasions his father laid hands on his mother. This devastated Colin. Admittedly, his father, unlike Daniel's, was not a bad person. It was the result of overwhelming stress and frustration – Mr Lee had been caught in the middle between his wife and mother who could not get along. Another contributing factor was Mrs Lee's gradual hearing loss due to ageing, which rendered effective communication between mother and son increasingly difficult. By and by, he became emotionally detached from his parents. Instead, he began to seek, and to give, his affection and attention outside of his family.

His first voluntary venture was with Tampines Home, a residential home under the Movement for the Intellectually Disabled Singapore (MINDS), for two hours weekly. The home was a misnomer in two ways – it was located at Thomson Road, not Tampines, and it had the vibes of a medical institution (not helped by its proximity to a hospital, a medical centre, and a hospice) rather than a home. Its residents were adults with intellectual disability, often the more severe kind, as well as those with other serious disabilities. It was not easy for the volunteers too, though many valiantly did their best under the circumstances, helping in physiotherapy sessions or providing meal-time entertainment. Some did lose steam and quit. In Colin's case, the morale-sapping low point came when his client, Bee Ching, whom he had been visiting faithfully and regularly for two years, simply forgot him after he had taken two weeks of medical leave to recover from chicken pox.

After Colin finished junior college and enlisted for National Service, he revisited Tampines Home and Bee Ching whenever he could find the time. One of his fellow volunteers there then recommended him to Chao Yang Special School, run by the Association for People with Special Needs (APSN) which also catered to persons with intellectual disability, but for those with higher levels of cognitive ability and functioning. Colin's impression of this school was that it was not so different from a mainstream primary school. Some of the students were even taught the preparatory modules for the PSLE. He was asked if he would be interested in giving tuition for the students, but after his experience with Tampines Home, he had this odd feeling of being out of place, and declined the offer. He wanted to contribute in other ways.

He found his calling in his freshman year in NTU with the Welfare Services Club. The Club was a varsity cooperative club that provided a range of voluntary and social service-related activities, from Regular Service Projects (RSPs in short), which served the elderly, youth, hearing impaired, visually handicapped and intellectually disabled, to ad-hoc charity fund-raising projects and public awareness carnivals. Immediately, he signed up for RSP (ID) which catered to Jurong Gardens School (JGS) graduates on Saturdays. Unlike Tampines Homes, RSP (ID)'s clients had moderate intellectual disability. They had been taught in school to be independent in daily-living activities, such as personal hygiene, self-expression and personal grooming skills. Half of these graduates from JGS, like Tim Soon, were referred to MINDS's employment development centres which provided sheltered employment. A few with higher cognitive ability might seek open employment through family contacts or Bizlink, a non-profit employment agency for the disabled. Regardless of their employment path, they needed to remain socially active to maintain their intellectual and general well-being. They were, after all, like anyone for whom a quality life encompasses not just work and home, but an active social life and leisure opportunities.

Saturdays, for most young people, usually mean a break from the toils of studies or work. But not for Colin and his fellow RSP (ID) volunteers. What they were doing was not easy either, especially for the new volunteers. People with intellectual disability might display behaviours which seem odd or unusual, such as talking to oneself, humming non-stop, or walking with an awkward gait. These took much getting used to, but with the help of their assigned mentor, the accustomisation process went smoothly.

Colin was paired with a trainee at the school who was four years his senior, but who had an intellectual development stage akin to that of a primary school kid. The trainee's cognitive strengths were in mathematics and language, so Colin and his mentor trained him in handling simple monetary transactions. Initially, they taught him simple counting up to thirty, using the abacus and fingers. After he grasped the concept of addition and subtraction, Colin taught him to use the pocket calculator to handle bigger numbers, much to his delight and fascination. When that too was accomplished, next up was the concept of money and change. This systematic, step-by-step approach to impart such knowledge took two years and required much patience and perseverance. Once, Colin dug out his trainee's old records and discovered, to his dismay, that he had, in fact, already learnt to count to one hundred some years ago. It was demoralising to realise the lack of coherent follow-ups and structured approach had been undermining his trainee's progress.

After graduating from NTU, Colin sought other avenues to volunteer. He joined the West End (WE) project which had been set up under the MINDS Youth Group. Like RSP (ID), West End worked with JGS to provide similar support for the students there, and became a natural progression for RSP (ID) volunteers to continue their work after they moved on from NTU.

Tim Soon was moving on too. Though he realised himself to be slower and different from others – the nice uncles at the hawker centre nearby always called him 'silly gourd' in Mandarin – he had hope and faith in himself. His dad had told him, when he was a kid, that he would go to school and then to work, just like others. At school, he had learnt about 'goals' from his teachers – goals were where you wanted yourself to be. And he had achieved his goal. As Mr Lee had taught him to say: *What's next?* Tim Soon didn't really know. Working at the centre at Margaret Drive suited him fine. With fellow trainees, Tim Soon was excitedly scrambling to put down his bag before taking his seat on one of the benches arranged in a semi-circle at the school canteen.

"Good afternoon, Mr Lee."

"Good afternoon Tim Soon. You had lunch?" Colin asked.

"Yes, Mr Lee."

"That's good. What you eat for lunch?"

"I eat rice and chicken. Vegetable and soup. Mummy cook."

"Very good," His trainee's reply was so forthcoming. "Ok, sit down here. We're starting singalong." That was the first activity of the afternoon for both WE and RSP (ID) trainees. Two volunteers went up to the front, ready to lead the group through songs such as *My Bonnie, Twinkle Twinkle Little Star, Edelweiss,* and more. When the related public holiday or occasion was nearing, they would sing *Da Di Hui Chun* (Tim Soon loved this one), *Stand up for Singapore,* or *We Wish You a Merry Christmas.*

"Good afternoon, everybody. My name is Miss Tan, and…"

"…I'm Mr Lim," The volunteers lightly tapped their right palms on their chests during their introductions, a gesture which served to boost the trainees' self-esteem. "Ok, who wants to sing the first song?" At this, there was an eruption of "Me! Me! Me!" from the enthusiastic trainees. "Ok, Mee Ling, you first. The rest can wait for the next song, ok?"

Mee Ling jumped up in excitement.

"Mee Ling, what you want to sing?"

"The Wheel of the Bus!"

At that, everyone got ready to move along with the song; they knew the actions by heart. "The wheel of the bus goes round and round, round and round, round and round …. all day long… The wiper of the bus goes sweep, sweep, sweep… The children of the bus goes up and down… all day long!"

Tim Soon sang along, his hands miming 'wheel', 'round', 'all day long'. Colin observed that a new trainee could not sync the actions in time; another was clapping when they sang 'sweep'. Even for those who had all the actions down pat, the pace and precision of their movements varied with their fine motor skills and coordination. They came to the last part of the song – singing 'up and down' – and on cue, everyone stood up and then sat down again in almost perfect unison. *Gross motor skills isn't a problem here,* Colin thought. The song ended with loud applause as Mee Ling, with a big smile on her face, returned to her seat.

Tim Soon was up next. When the third song was offered, it was followed by Lien who had Down Syndrome. He did not really know any lyrics nor could he sing, but he had raised his hand anyway. Mr Lim asked him to step up and prompted, "Lien, shall we sing *Old MacDonald has a farm?*" Lien nodded. The song started. Miss Tan and Mr Lim led the singing while Lien was contented to gaze around at his fellow trainees. Nobody minded. Again, a generous round of applause accompanied Lien as he went back to his seat, brimming with pride and elation.

Twenty minutes and eight songs later, Miss Tan announced, "Now, we'll give out your name tags. When we call your name, come up here to collect it. Ok? Mee Ling."

Mee Ling stood and walked right next to Miss Tan who asked, "What is your name?" Mee Ling placed her right palm on her chest and tapped it as she replied, "My name is Mee Ling." Everyone clapped. Miss Tan passed the name tag to her. Colin noticed that Tim Soon was looking puzzled, and thought perhaps he was wondering why this routine was needed when almost all his fellow trainees already knew each other through school or work. Tim Soon was certainly sharp enough to think of this, and Colin, in turn, mused for a moment how he could explain the exercise was to enhance the trainees' self confidence and social skills. But he put it out of his mind as the next activity started. Everyone had already spilt into their respective groups, ready to start on their sessions proper.

As people with intellectual disability tend to face difficulty in integrating with the larger society because of their behavioural presentations, there was much effort put into working with them on this aspect. Behaviour modification strategies vary depending on the individual trainee's level of functioning, communication ability and attention span.

"Good afternoon trainees, I'm Mr Lee and this is Ms Wong," Colin commenced the class with his fellow volunteer, Jessica. "Today we'll learn about the correct behaviours when taking a public bus. Before we begin, we must decide on two simple rules all of us have to follow." Colin was pointing to a flip-chart as he went over the two points. No talking when others are talking. If you don't understand, raise your hand and ask; it's perfectly ok. Colin made sure he explained these clearly and slowly. Then the lights dimmed and photos and slides were projected – visual aids helped with complex concepts. Colin and Jessica also quizzed the trainees now and then to retain their attention.

In the middle of the session, one trainee, Meg, suddenly stood up and started yelling. "Argggghhh!" Startled, every head turned towards her. Meg stopped shouting, looking pleased with herself and remained standing. At this, Colin walked up to Meg and looked her in the eye, but she avoided his glaze.

"Meg. Meg!" Finally, she made eye contact. "Meg, remember the rule? No one should talk or shout when others are talking. You are also disturbing your friends. If you shout again, you will have to leave your friends and stand in the corridor outside for fifteen minutes. You understand?" Meg meekly nodded her headed and sat down.

But ten minutes later, Meg repeated her antics, only this time, she yelled longer and louder. Jessica went over to her, looking stern. "Meg, look at me. You disturbed everyone again. Come with me outside. You will not be with your friends here. They need to listen to the lecture. Come with me." She grabbed Meg by her wrist and showed her to the door. Meg teared up but followed silently. They walked out from the classroom to a spot visible from the door. There, Jessica told Meg to face the door.

"Stand here for fifteen minutes quietly. Don't turn your head too. I'll come fetch you when time's up. Meanwhile, try to remember what Mr Lee said about proper behaviour on the bus. I'll ask you later." Redirection was an effective tool in managing misbehaviour.

Meg could only nod. Now she regretted acting out. She was alone and felt like crying, but she knew nobody was listening to or watching her. Meg wanted to scream and yell too, but that would make things worse – her tea break might be delayed or, worse, her parents might be told not to bring her here next week. She liked the activities here.

Mm, what did Mr Lee say just now? Oh, we should not raise our voices on the bus because it was a public place and we might disturb others. About being considerate. Everyone loves considerate girls and boys, right? No wonder Ms Wong was upset. It took Meg only a short while to realise these and decide the best course of action was to tough out the rest of the quiet time, and think about the nice things Ms Wong would say to her when she returned. Ms Wong always praised her if she accepted her punishment without complaint. Always.

CONVERSIONS

I t wasn't like this.

By now, Thursday had lost its allure – the denizens of the Singapore Boys' Home, except for a handful, treated it like any normal weekday. Once, Block E would be thrown into a frenzy when the NTU volunteers turned up. The boys would mash their faces onto the room windows on the third and fourth floors, wolf-whistle at the female volunteers and call out their names. Even before their arrival in the evening, the teasing would start – the boys who participated in the programme, which included the Privileged Three, would have it bad. Some of the non-participating ones also conjured ways to badger the new volunteers to bring in forbidden magazines and items.

Peter, Wee Kiang and Daniel had the older boys telling them, "Tell those goons the only currency traded here are 'reading materials'. If they don't bring us what we want, then we won't join in their silly activities." Wee Kiang and Daniel ignored them, but Peter and the other two boys from the adjacent wards often succeeded in securing scratchbooks with idol pictures, pop lyrics and even printouts of fan-club chatroom transcripts.

"How the hell could those so-called smart university people be so easily tricked?" Daniel mused to Wee Kiang one day, to which the latter replied, "Well, those greenhorns are desperate to make us open up to them, to get into our good books. That's how and why. Besides, those ignorant students would never dream some of those materials they brought in contained the codes that Peter and his gangs needed. Keep this to yourself, but rumour has it that a female volunteer was made use of, years ago, to unknowingly deliver 'secret mails' out of the Girls' Home. It came to light when the RO stumbled across the girl's cupboard. The poor volunteer was politely asked to leave." Upon hearing this, Daniel could only heave a disgusted sigh.

Daniel himself had initially not taken to his befriender – their interactions were, at best, superficial and patronising. At its worst, it had threatening undertones. To Daniel, his befriender's biggest demerit was the fact that he was an adult. And adults absolutely could not be trusted. To make things worse, he was plain boring and preachy, and kept talking about himself, his student life in NTU and probing into Daniel's private matters and his past. This only served to dredge up unpleasant memories which he wanted to forget, thank you very much.

Worse of all, Victor had lied – Daniel knew it. Victor claimed he had no sister during their very first meeting. Daniel could tell from his eyes and the hesitant way he denied it. Now, why had he done that? Did he think Daniel might hound her in future? *What an insult! Were all adults unable to be truthful or sincere, like those parents who came during Save-Face Days?*

But that was then.

This was now – there had been an unexpected and complete change in how he saw things. It was as if the firm ground under his feet had given way and he had fallen through into another reality. Victor, during their latest session, had revealed everything about his sister, Wai Leng – her illness and suffering, his family's struggles and fractures, his own guilt and agony. Why Victor had poured his heart out like that, Daniel had no idea. But he believed Victor's account – his sorrow could not be faked. Daniel finally understood why Victor had lied about not having a sister. In fact, he could grasp it was pretty much the same reason he had not told anyone, even Wee Kiang, about his broken family.

Daniel found himself, to his surprise and discomfort, at a loss. He did not know how he was supposed to feel – compassion for Victor? But he didn't want to feel that way. *No*, he told himself, *I don't feel sorry for him or his family.* But what exactly made him keep thinking of Victor and his trauma? Was it empathy? Or something else? He couldn't understand this either – Victor had indeed experienced the vicissitudes of life. Just like Daniel himself. Yet he seemed to have coped with it better, and had somehow found a way to move on. He had, in fact, started helping others and even took on the thankless work of volunteering with difficult people like Daniel. Why?

He intended to find out.

The sessions had undergone two changes: there were now groups of four – two volunteers and two boys in each group – in a bid to increase positive interactions. Most reading materials were also banned from the sessions. Most of the boys welcomed the first move; for them, it was double the action and half the boredom, and they also like the fact they had a peer with them during the sessions. The latter change met with grunts of disapproval though, and at first, they continued to clamour for their weekly dose of *Cleo* or *I-Weekly*. But these gradually ceased as Shafid's idea of organising group activities such as mind-mapping exercises and word puzzles contests managed to engage the boys. They also started to have more interesting conversations. As luck had it, Daniel found himself paired with Wee Kiang, his best pal in Block E, and Wee Kiang's befriender, Susan.

"Wee Kiang, read through this chapter of the physics textbook first. I'm sorry, but I need to go over to see how the other volunteers are coping. I'll be back soon to help you with the exercises." And off she would go, darting from group to group to check on each one. Wee Kiang understood his volunteer doubled up as a coordinator, so he did not mind and obediently revised his work. A tutor to help him prepare for his GCE 'O' Levels was more than what he could ask for, and he was grateful. Such an arrangement was fine for Daniel too, for Wee Kiang's presence lightened the atmosphere and Susan's intermittent absence also provided chances for Daniel to find out more about Victor. This time, he started the conversation, for the first time in so many months.

"Why don't Susan just leave Wee Kiang to another NTU student, instead of having to run around?" Daniel asked. But Wee Kiang was too engrossed in his studies that he did not pay attention to what was being said.

"Cos there're not enough volunteers. Besides, I'd do that too if I were her. No point being here if we only do coordinating work. We volunteers want to do something more meaningful by having our own attached boy to work with," Victor replied, and instantly regretted using the word 'attached', perhaps implying possessiveness and superiority. "I'm sure all of us, the coordinator included, wish to be real friends with you guys. That's why we're here."

"Ha. Really? You mean try to make us good boys? I say we don't need that."

That did it. Victor snapped. "Stop being so cynical and make us sound so noble. We aren't your counsellors nor saviours, and we never claimed to be. We're volunteers. We just want to help. And being able to help makes us happy, so why not? Life is already hard enough, no matter where we are. Why make it harder for us and for yourselves?"

Daniel was slightly taken aback. His soft-spoken volunteer must be really worked up to become so fierce. In spite of himself, he began to feel a certain degree of admiration for the chap for putting up with him and his taunting. Now he was curious. *No harming probing eh?* "But what makes you want to make friends with me? We are practically strangers. I mean, you didn't even treat your own sister that nice."

Victor looked at him, eyes wide and deadly serious. He then took a deep breath and said, his voice barely above a whisper. "That's my life's greatest regret. I let her down. I let my mum down. And this made me seek the meaning of life, seek to understand the value of life, and how making a difference to others' lives is the most meaningful thing we can do."

Again, despite himself, Daniel was touched. Victor did not seem to be preaching, but rather, talking to himself, even berating himself.

"What keeps me hanging on when what I do is unappreciated? It's remorse. I figured that since that was how I treated my sister back then, what's so big a deal about being given the cold shoulder now? I had hoped to make life better for both her and you, but I didn't know how then. When I finally knew, for my sister, it was too late. I can never make it up to her. But I hope I can do something for you, and I hope you stay on in this programme."

Suddenly, Wee Kiang, whom Daniel thought had been engrossed with his homework, put down his pen, looked up and told them: "Don't worry, I'll make sure Daniel carry on with this programme."

Daniel grinned then. "Yes. Why should I quit? It feels good having an undergraduate to talk to. I'm the envy of all the others. You know what they call Peter, Wee Kiang and I? The. Privileged. Three. Cool huh? Right, Wee Kiang?"

"You bet!" Wee Kiang winked.

Victor finally smiled. "Thanks, guys. You know what they say about strangers? They are just people you've yet to know."

"Like us?" Daniel rejoined, confirming the ice had melted. They were still strangers, but getting less so all the time.

Three tables away, Susan was saying to another group. "Excuse me, but I got to return to Wee Kiang and checked on his answers. He's pretty tense up over the scary Os, ya know?"

Since 1962, the Movement for Intellectually Disabled of Singapore, more popularly known as MINDS, has been running twelve centres, two residential homes, three employment development centres, two training and development centres and five special education schools. By 2004, most of its facilities and buildings were old and looked run-down. Except one. The new Margaret Drive MINDS building was stylishly designed and colourful; it was nestled within the green belt of

Alexandra Road. Costing more than eight million dollars – Singapore International Airlines (SIA) sponsored half of it – it was MINDS' biggest employment centre. The six-storey building also housed the MINDS headquarters and Employment Development Centre (EDC).

About 370 persons with intellectual disability worked in the sheltered workshops, of which 70% manned the SIA production lines on the second and third floors. The national airline had been MINDS' biggest corporate sponsor since the 1990s, and had outsourced its headset repackaging work to MINDS. Every day, a truck would arrive at the EDC's loading bay to drop off twenty-five thousand used headsets. These were then moved to the centre's seven production units. At each unit – varying from twenty to fifty plus clients – the headsets were sorted, disentangled, disinfected, sealed and packed anew.

Over the years, SIA-MINDS EDC also developed social enterprise projects to provide employment opportunities for MINDS clients. Those not on the SIA production lines took on other in-house projects like operating the cafeteria on the ground floor and providing sanitary and cleaning services. About two dozen clients who showed talent in the arts were assigned to the Art and Craft section on the fourth floor. There, they hand-made beautifully painted glass or wooden frames, pressed bookmarks and all sorts of handicrafts which were sold to corporates or schools. There were also other projects, which roped in volunteer parents and patrons, such as a new MINDS catering service, and the MINDS Thrift Shops operated by the Singapore Armed Forces' Officers Wives Club and a group of European ladies selling donated products at low prices. Such were the efforts of the Open Employment Committee and its corporate partners; for example, BP-Merrill Lynch undertook a manual carwash project at Pasir Panjang BP petrol kiosk, Bizlink and Singapore Polytechnic initiated window-cleaning and domestic cleaning projects.

Only the income generated from the open employment jobs went directly to the clients. For in-house projects such as the SIA contract and the cafeteria enterprise, the clients were paid according to four grades based on the Training Officers' evaluations of each client's performance. As a voluntary welfare organisation (VWO) supported by the National Council of Social Service, the grants, funding and donations had to be accounted for and properly audited. MINDS had a multi-disciplinary team of qualified training officers, social workers, occupational therapists, physiotherapists, speech therapists and psychologists.

On that day, a delegation from Hong Kong happened to be paying a visit to EDC to observe how the centre was run. Let's follow them to learn more about the center and its clients. At the station where the repackaging of headsets for Singapore's flagship airline was, the clients were being taught basic workplace safety processes, such as proper handling of the Dettol swap for sanitising and the right posture to adopt when carrying heavy cartons. All well and good.

But trouble struck soon after. When one young lady from the delegation commended a client on his good work attitude, he was quick to grab her hands, shocking her. "Shaq, you're not supposed to do that to the lady. It's improper," one of the staff stepped in. *What's the matter?* Shaq wondered. He liked the lady. *It was so nice of her to praise me, so why couldn't I express my liking?*

"Shaq, if you wish to thank this lady for her nice words, then you shouldn't grab her hands like that just now. You should say 'thank you' instead. Understand?" The lady, recovering from her initial shock, added, "That's right, Shaq. You are already very good with sealing these headphones. You will be a better worker if you say 'thank you' politely when other people praise you. Come, I'd very much like to hear that from you."

Shaq uttered a soft 'thank you' and then broke into a toothy smile. He repeated, "Thank you, teacher."

"You're welcome, Shaq."

For those with intellectual disability, it was a challenge to teach them or make them fully understand which behaviours were inappropriate. This case was fortunately straightforward, but others were much more difficult to handle, such as incidents of self-stimulation and mutual masturbation among clients at the workplace. After all, they too underwent puberty and experienced the same sexual desires and urges as anyone else, but they might not grasp the concept of privacy and social norms which frown on such explicit expressions of their sexuality.

SONG-SIGNS

Though unfamiliar to the general public, song-signing is not that much different from a piece of musical or contemporary choir performance. Song signers, like singers, memorise the lyrics, spend time and effort to rehearse, and finally get to perform on stage. Song-signing is about movement, based on sign language, to express the sentiments of the particular song.

Song signers usually sign in a stylised manner to the flow of the melody and lyrics as the song plays. For deaf song signers, they follow the rhythm of the music, that is, for those who are able to hear the music, however imperfectly, using their hearing aids. Or they depend on a 'reflector' – a hearing person who faces them and song-signs along to cue them. Song signing could be performed to any pop song, even Christmas carols, as long as the performer comes up with the choreography for it. And as how a talented singer could convey the mood of a song with vocal prowess and soulful delivery, so too a good song-signer could bring forth the same emotion through body language and facial expressions. Dance steps could even be incorporated in the song-signing performance – which made for an unique visual feast indeed.

Venue: At the Library@Esplanade
Date: 18 December 2004
Event: Musical "A Christmas Celebration" by a song-signing group from SADeaf

Rachel:

Good evening, ladies and gentlemen. Welcome to our play! Presented by the Singapore Association for the Deaf, this show aims to promote awareness and understanding of deaf people among the public. The story is about Britney, who is deaf. Please sit back and enjoy!

Scene One

> *Parents watching TV in the living room. Britney alone in her room reading a magzine.*

> *Britney looks bored, puts on her hearing aid, and turns on the radio. She frowns, looks exasperated, twists something on her hearing aid and squints in concentration. Shaking her head, she turns up the radio's volume. The sounds emitting from the radio becomes louder and louder.*

> *Parents in living room look at each other. The father nudges his wife. She goes to Britney's room and says something to her. Britney turns down the volume, looking unhappy. After a while, she stomps out of the*

*room. Her parents continue watching TV and ignore
her. She angrily leaves the house.*

(Exit stage left. Curtains down.)

Scene Two

*The stage shows the inside of a mall, with a Christmas
tree in the middle. The song 'White Christmas' plays in
the background. Two girls, arm in arm, are shopping
and enjoying the festive atmosphere. Britney enters stage
left. She is crying.*

Chandice:	Hey Britney! What happened? Why are you crying?
Britney:	I'm upset with my parents. It's so hard to communicate with them!
Chandice:	That reminds me! We have something to show you.
Linda:	Yes, yes, come with us! Promise you'll like it!

*The trio walk a big round along the perimeter of the
stage, ending at the center. As they walk, a group of six
carollers walk out and stand in front of the Christmas
tree. The carollers then begin to song sign along as 'Hark
the Herald Angels Sing' plays.*

*Britney stops short when she sees the performance. Her
face is a picture of surprise and joy.*

(As the song comes to an end, the curtains go down.)

Scene Three

At a cafe, around a table.

Britney: Hi Rachel and Fannie, happy to meet you. And thanks to Linda and Chandice for introducing us. I heard you're from the Singapore Association for the Deaf?

Rachel: Actually, my fellow carollers and I are volunteers with the association. We are members of its performing arm. But Fannie here works for the association.

Chandice: Oh? What services does the association provide? We know very little about it actually.

Fannie: Well, we have services like sign language interpretation for our deaf clients, family support, hearing care, and early intervention for children diagnosed with hearing loss. To reach out to the public, we conduct sign language courses and awareness workshops too.

Britney: That's interesting.

Colin: You are a student at Boon Lay Secondary School? Are you doing ok in school?

Britney: Quite ok. I'm deaf, but my classmates do not see me as any different from them. I have some good friends too, like Linda and Chandice here.

Chandice: I think sign language is cool. We picked up some signs from Britney.

Britney: The teachers are very nice too. Sometimes I can't catch what they're saying, and they are very patient with me.

Linda: That's right. As long as they speak clearly and not rattle away, Britney is able to cope in school.

Colin:	That's amazing. But how do you understand them? Do you lip read?
Britney:	No, I can't lip read. But it helps my understanding of speech if I can see the speaker's face. I use hearing aids to amplify sounds. But my parents are Chinese-educated, while I only learnt English. So we have problems communicating.
Fannie:	Maybe you can approach the association for help. I can link you up with the relevant staff there.
Chandice:	Can we join in your carolling project too?
Rachel:	Yes, you are welcome to!
Britney:	Can I get my parents to join in too?
Rachel:	Of course, they are very welcome!

Scene Four

The words 'A year later.' are projected on the backdrop. It fades.

Mall scene from Scene Two is reenacted.

Everyone is on stage, including Britney, her parents, Linda and Chandice, in front of the Christmas tree. 'Silver Bells' starts to play and the carollers sign along with joy.

Rachel:	I hope all of you have enjoyed our Christmas play this evening. On behalf of the National Library Board and everyone here, we hope you have a good evening and wishing a Merry Christmas to all. Thank you!

"The response was fantastic. A pity the venue was too small. Imagine the sensation it'd create if we had performed at the outdoor stage at the Esplanade!" Colin said. Rachel was silent. She was walking with Colin along the bank of the Singapore River, after a sumptuous dinner celebration with her carolling team.

Colin continued speaking. "Don't you agree? I think this play helped educate the public in many more ways than a mass song signing would. I like that dialogue at the cafe in particular. How wonderful if the play can reach more people. Come to think of it, Britney is pretty fortunate for a person with disability. Ok, I should say people with disability are not necessarily unfortunate people, but it's really good to see how deaf people can lead normal lives and are largely socially accepted. At least compared to those with intellectual disability, cerebral palsy or Down Syndrome."

Rachel finally broke her silence. "I doubt in most cases, the deaf receive as much acceptance or understanding as you'd like to think. Take Joanne – she has certainly gone through many rough patches throughout her schooling years. It wasn't as rosy as Britney's when it comes to being accepted by lecturers or tutors or classmates. Joanne does have good friends and lecturers, but they are the exception rather than the norm."

A sampan floated down the Singapore River from a distance as they stopped and stood by the riverside. "So it's not so different for her or any other deaf student, is it?" Colin mused aloud. "It's the same with intellectual disability. We go on and on educating the public about those with intellectual disability, what they can do and what they cannot, and try so hard to persuade people to help them integrate into society, but.. the fact is, most employers only measure the worth of a person based on their own narrow definition of ability. For the deaf, at least the attitude seems to be 'Never mind. As long as you can be educated, you can still be a useful person.' Why can't it be 'Never mind if you have intellectual disability, you can still work'?"

Rachel was thoughtful. "Human nature? Ignorance? Perhaps it's because deaf people's deafness is invisible, and they can behave in 'normal' ways. So people are more at ease and comfortable around them. Compared to the intellectually disabled who might display odd behaviours in public."

Colin cut in, "But intellectual development and public behaviour are linked. If you are cognitively high-functioning, you will likely be familiar with the concept of social norms."

"Oh well, it depends. It's not so simple. There are many factors at play here."

Then the conversation took a hundred-and-eighty-degree turn.

"So have you thought about our marriage?" Rachel asked.

Colin was stupefied. True, it had been on his mind since he knew her. But he never expected her to bring it up this way.

"But I thought you said it's more important we focus on developing our careers first?"

"I also said career's only half the reason, and the other half was that we needed to see Joanne and Tim Soon through their milestone life stages. They are both doing fine now in NTU and EDC, aren't they? So there's only half a valid reason, which is no reason at all."

So Rachel was being Rachel, with such a sense of illogical logic, Colin thought. But he agreed with her. They had done a lot for others over the past two years, and it was time they thought about themselves.

FALL-OUT

Despite his relatively modest financial situation, Mr Foo did not feel his life was poor in any way. At least he had a coach, the one he was driving now, which he could ferry his family around when his schedule permitted. He felt proud of his family, and of how he could earn a living all those years, and of his capable wife who had worked just as hard to bring up the children and manage the household. There were also his children of course, Tim Soon and Tim Mei, who had been – by God's blessing – healthy and happy.

True, the Foos could have lamented how cruel fate had been to them regarding Tim Soon. But even with his disability, the boy was, blessedly, more discerning and mature than many of his peers. Did his intellectual disability spare him the unwholesome temptations and vices so prevalent in society, or had Heaven watched over him more to make up for his disadvantages? Mr Foo often read in the papers how the youth of today were becoming more willful and behaving badly. At least his children were turning out well, he thought, as he headed for the heavy vehicle park in the falling light.

There had been one problem, though, which was his daughter's initial rejection of her elder brother, and which had ended up, on many occasions, in quarrels and unhappiness. To put the blame on Tim Mei, however, would not be reasonable, for how could the young girl understand fully what her elder brother's condition meant? The thought of going through all these was tough enough for adults, let alone a child. During her pre-teen years, she did not receive any support from the community and was not informed about her brother's condition either.

Mr Foo recalled an incident on Tim Soon's eleventh birthday, when Tim Mei had dragged her mother aside and asked why he had so much difficulty counting the candles on the cake. She could only say, "Mei Mei, when God made Soon, he forgot to put in a part of his brain that deals with counting. So he's slower." They had not realised that by failing to give Tim Mei the full picture, she had ended up feeling only embarrassment instead of empathy, and she didn't want a part in it. She also lacked the skills, techniques and knowledge to interact with her brother properly. Mr Foo was relieved he had enrolled his family into the MINDS Parents & Sibling Support Group upon Colin's recommendation, which had done much to help Tim Mei come to terms with her brother.

After a good chat with the social workers, Tim Mei and her parents had been persuaded to attend the support sessions at MINDS once every three weeks. Mr and Mrs Foo had learnt about the importance of good communication with not just Tim Soon, but also the need to bring Tim Mei into the loop. They learnt that their daughter needed to be given age-appropriate information about the disability. They met and shared with other families in the same situation, and realised they were not alone, which did wonders to help Tim Mei develop a positive attitude towards her brother. In short, the support group was a platform for the Foo family to bond together in the midst of adversity.

Mr Foo smiled to himself. The curtain of darkness was being drawn, but Mr Foo knew the roads like the back of his hands. In the approaching twilight, he felt his age and also thought of something else. As parents, Mr Foo and his wife had always taken upon themselves the responsibility to raise and support Tim Foo for as long as they lived. They had been consumed by the day-by-day struggles and concerns of looking after Tim Soon, and of how their son would cope with life at home and in school.

But one day Tim Mei had asked, "What happens to us when both of you are gone? You should start to plan for that future." Mrs Foo had replied, "What planning do you have in mind? Soon is already independent, isn't he? Don't you worry. It's your free choice how you would be involved when we are gone. There is no obligation." *This must surely have confused Tim Mei,* Mr Foo thought, *for how could we tell her that, after so much effort to bring her closer to her brother. How could Tim Mei ever be able to cast off her brother to live her own life?* If Mr Foo were in her shoes, he definitely could not.

He finally drove the coach to the parking lot. Then it happened. Mr Foo had been distracted by the never-ending worries about his family and his attention drifted. Reversing to manoeuvre his coach into the parking spot, he did not see the oncoming lorry. The only things Mr Foo could remember, much later, was a loud crash, his side door caving in, and a bone-rattling pain in his right shoulder, before his world became darkness.

Three Gems

"I find life an exciting business and most exciting when it is lived for others."

Helen Keller

SECOND JOB

Mr Foo suffered a broken collarbone and concussion. The accident also cost him his job. The transport company was kind enough to add three months' pay to the severance package in view of his long service, but Mr Foo could not hope to use his right upper limb for a good part of an entire year for any task more strenuous than lifting a pot.

Tim Mei was worried – about her father and about the family finances. She pondered taking up a part-time job, but that might affect her studies and her finals were only two months away. She knew her father would refuse to let her work because of that. Her mother was a good seamstress and could do some sewing to supplement Tim Soon's meagre allowance from the EDC. But time to a housewife was a scarce commodity made scarcer by her husband's dependence on her for some of his mobility needs. The family could only hope Tim Soon could get an open employment job with a bigger pay cheque to tide them over.

And only one person could help her elder brother in this endeavour.

When Colin received the bad news from Tim Mei, he was scrubbing the toilet at home. That was his ritual every weekend if he didn't have standby duties. Colin was the rare breed of volunteer who held a dim view of overseas community service projects – those which involved school repairs, road reparation projects and such in developing countries. *Did they think spending money and air mileage mean greater involvement? Or was that by doing so, you would be branded as a kind-hearted person?* Colin figured it must be a mixture of several reasons, all of which he disagreed with. Colin's philosophy was simply this: *If you can't squeeze out one or two hours weekly to do your share for your family, then how could you justify the far longer time spent on others?* So, he volunteered for the weekly chores of toilet cleaning and ironing clothes.

After he said goodbye to Tim Mei and put down the phone, what arose in his mind, oddly, was the image of his own father, whom he had disliked since he was young. Yet, Mr Foo's accident hit him hard and was an awakening of sorts. *Life is so unpredictable – any moment could be our last. What if I departed this world with regrets, as in not making up with my estranged loved ones?* On that Sunday evening, in the toilet, Colin sat still for a long time, thinking it over.

The next morning, Colin rolled up his sleeves and got to work. With Mr Foo's permission, he called Bizlink, a non-profit placement agency for people with disabilities. After relating Soon's background and his family plight, he was referred to the Employment Placement Division, where an appointment was made with the Foo family. According to Bizlink, there were three broad categories of disabilities: sensory disabilities referring to hearing and visual impairment; intellectually/learning disabilities that included ID, autism spectrum disorder and attention deficit hyperactivity disorder; and finally physical disabilities. Depending on the extent of disability, the person with disability could be trained to handle a wide range of jobs, especially if employers were prepared to make certain modifications to the job scope and workplace facilities.

On the day of the Bizlink appointment, Colin was with the Foos to help them find out more. The jobs considered ideal for those with intellectual disability incorporated tasks which were repetitive and routine. Examples of such jobs were dishwashers, packers, F&B crew, cleaners, to name a few. Tim Mei asked for the best paying position, which turned out to be for a room steward position at Sheraton Towers. Although a bit daunted by the prospect of Tim Soon taking on such seemingly complicated work, they agreed to give him a chance to try out for it. It helped that Tim Soon was assessed to be a good fit, possessing an inclination towards mathematics and language.

Bizlink followed up when concerns arose. Sheraton Towers already hired some disabled people among its stable of chambermaids, laundry operators and technicians. But few had intellectual disability and Sheraton was a five-star hotel of international repute, so it took some convincing that Tim Soon could manage the rooms as with any other steward. Tim Soon had to sign up for the on-the-job training service provided by Bizlink's training officer during his training phase with the chief steward. The training officer helped promote a better awareness of Tim Soon's disability among his colleagues and showcased his ability. This led to better acceptance of him and established a working rapport between them. The officer also facilitated adjustments to his job scope, explained what was needed and why to the chief steward.

For example, the service menu was simplified for Tim Soon, with the verbose words replaced by pictorial diagrams. Another redesign was adjusting the choices on the order form in the alphabetic sequence, so that Tim Soon could form the associations better. It worked. By the end of the one-month training phase, Tim Soon had secured a job with slightly shorter shift hours, helpful and accommodating colleagues, and a very proud chief steward who was praised by her boss for successfully integrating Tim Soon.

Tim Soon himself took the experience positively; he had been trained to meet each of his new goals in life in that manner. To him, as with many people with disabilities, it was not merely a job, but a symbol of independence and achievement. He also had no inferiority complex nor lack of confidence, for he believed there would always be wonderful people like his teachers and volunteers like Colin in his world to guide him. He might fail at times, but he never stopped trying, and in the end, he always made it and managed to earn his keep.

"Listen! George, listen!"

George leaned forward and tapped his fingers against his cheeks to indicate that he was listening. George was three years old and had profound hearing loss in both ears. A year ago, he underwent cochlear implant surgery for his left ear, in which a magnetic receiver was implanted into the mastoid bone in the skull to receive digitally coded signals from an external sound processor.

Upon his diagnosis, his parents had gone through a long period of grief and guilt. George was fitted with his very first pair of hearing aids. But he still struggled to progress in his communication skills, hence the resort to the implant. Technically speaking, George could hear with his implant, but he was still missing out on certain softer and high-frequency speech sounds. He was also not alert to surrounding sounds. The audiologist then referred George to attend Auditory Verbal Therapy (AVT) sessions at a hospital. His parents received a subsidy and only had to pay 10% of the session fees. With weekly AVT sessions, George was able to learn to hear a greater variety of speech and environmental sounds.

"What is this, George?" Rachel asked.

The little boy gave a cheeky smile. His mother shrugged, refusing his request for prompts. George frowned as he thought very hard.

Suddenly, he sat up and, with a wide smile on this face, shouted, "THIS IS A HIPPOPOTAMUS!"

Mummy clapped, the therapist clapped, George beamed with pride.

"Oh Rachel! I didn't know George could say hippopotamus!"

"Yes, Helen. And he did it so well. Remember we were working on his 't' sound and his final 's'? He got them all today! It's wonderful! Good job, mummy."

Rachel added, "You have worked very hard with George. Okay! We have had enough for today. See you all next week! And remember all the homework you have to do. Continue doing therapy at home."

It had been three years since Rachel first stumbled upon this position advertised in the papers. She had applied and had no regrets – the work had brought her a lot of joy, though it often brought her heartache too. The joy came when the patients surprised her with their progress, the heartache when they did not. Being an AVT was not so different from being a school teacher or social worker, Rachel had thought, if you considered the job scope. She worked not just with the patient, but hand in hand with the doctors, the audiologists, the parents, and the school teachers too. Goals had to be set for each patient, lesson plans had to be drawn up, and things sometimes got messy, and she had to counsel the parents when they felt discouraged or when they did not put in enough effort in their child's rehabilitation. Sometimes, the children had behavioural problems or other medical conditions which had to be tackled on the spot.

The most challenging cases, Rachel felt, were children with multiple disabilities or medical conditions, which required much modifications of the techniques used. It was a job where you had to be on the ball – aggressive when managing the patient, and compassionate and empathetic to understand the needs of the child and their parents. To Rachel, every day was a learning experience. While her patients were learning to listen, she was learning from them and their parents too. Having a deaf child was no easy task but the parents generally took it in good stride.

Besides, Rachel very much enjoyed what she was doing, and had seen quite a number of her patients learning to speak well and coping in schools. George was one of her first patients, and she had watched him grow from a little baby to this handsome toddler. Nothing could be more rewarding than to know she had played a part in this.

That happened.

And at about the same time George was discharged a year later, Bizlink's services was called upon once more. Rachel Khoo found she was taking up a similar responsibility to search a suitable employment for Joanne, after her graduation. The tutor's kind intent was merely to increase Joanne's chance of a job offer, but her effort was not well-received, and sparked fierce objection from Joanne herself. She wanted to strike it out on her own, and take up a job like others', not one meant for people with disability. She wanted a job that allowed her to communicate with people, to listen and speak. Joanne didn't want to choose a career and life where she needed to hide her disability, but to show it openly to others without fear, and with strength and courage.

FORGIVENESS

Daniel Lok stepped into the Toa Payoh Swimming Complex and was utterly enchanted, and also bewildered. Everything seemed so familiar – the sounds, sights and smells of the place where he had spent so much time during his teenage years: the blue water in the two Olympic-sized pools that smelt heavily of chlorine; the spectator stand in the middle, boasting comfortable polyester green seats mounted on rows of wooden planks, shaded partially by a grand overhanging roof; people in swim gear dotted in and around the perimeters of the pools. It was more hectic and crowded than usual that day – there were lifeguards, timekeepers, uniformed staff, float lines strung across the pool lanes, audio speakers which came to life now and then and drowning out the noise from the crowd, and huge colourful banners pinned up all over, among which the largest proclaimed "MINISTRY SWIMMING MEET 2005".

For some time, Daniel stood where he was, taking in the scene as if it was an extraterrestrial sight. His heart skipped a beat when he spotted the rows of glistering trophies and medals neatly arranged on the table in the middle front of the stand. It was all real; he was really taking part in the swimming competition. He closed his eyes for a minute and relived the countless times he had been there, and thought of his swim mates who went through so much with him in training and in competitions all those years ago. He slowly opened his eyes slowly and took a deep breath. He was finally back where he wanted to be, thanks to Victor and his Youth befrienders.

After Victor had shared about his sister, Daniel had likewise started to open up about himself and his life – his family issues, school woes and passion for swimming. He had not expected Victor to approach the Home's management with a proposal, which was then forwarded to the ministry's Rehabilitation and Protection Division which ran with the idea. And this was the eventual outcome, and a delightful one.

"Ladies and gentlemen," the public address speaker blared. "Welcome to the Ministry of Community, Youth and Sports Swimming Meet cum Family Day 2005. This is the very first year we have combined our annual family day with a special event – a swimming meet organised by the Singapore Boys' Home, for the best swimmers from each of the Home's four blocks. After that, all of you are invited for a buffet lunch reception prepared by the newly formed MINDS Catering Service at the stadium side. Meanwhile, please continue to be seated while the swimmers assemble at the registration counter for a briefing."

The announcement lifted Daniel. He felt as if he was floating as he made his way to the counter. He did not care about winning or trophies or glory. He just wanted to swim again. At the counter, he eyed his fellow swimmers. They had well-toned, lanky bodies and exuded confidence – worthy opponents indeed. And then, for a fleeting instant, Daniel thought he saw a familiar face before it vanished into the crowd, and stopped short in surprise.

Was it him? No way. It couldn't be. He must have seen wrongly.

By ten o'clock, the spectator stand was full. Turning out in force were staff from the Home and ministry, volunteers, families of the Home residents, and VIPs. Unlike the others, Wee Kiang was not looking forward to the carnival when their families would show up. His 'O' Level examination was just round the corner, and he would rather spend the remaining time studying. But he wanted to show his support for Daniel.

Just then, in the midst of the crowd, he heard his name being called. He turned and there his father and mother stood, looking at him expectantly. Surprise robbed him of speech. *The old man definitely looked more haggard since his last visit,* Wee Kiang thought as his parents approached. His mother looked hale and hearty, and had made the effort to dress up for the occasion. But her halting gait betrayed her hip trouble. Wee Kiang briefly experienced a pang of sadness – his parents had grown older and frailer. But he turned bitter again. *Well, they have their precious daughter to take care of them.*

"Hi, son," his father said, reaching out to pat Wee Kiang's shoulder. "I'm sorry we're late. This cursed leg of mine acted up again this morning. It has been some time since we met. You look good all the same. We got to know you'll be having your exams in two weeks' time. How's everything?" Wee Kiang's mother simply looked happy to see him and kept smiling at him. He felt something in him thaw towards his parents. He said, "The competition is starting soon. Let's find seats first."

At the poolside, the swimmers were limbering up, raring to go, Daniel among them. As one, they stepped up to the platform, adjusted their googles, and got ready. Daniel stole glances at his opponents and.. no way! It really was Mark! Just three lanes away from him. From his lane assignment, Mark was representing the Home too. Daniel was stunned, his mind thrown into turmoil. *What the..? Why and when was Mark sent to SBH?*

Then a blast of the horn and a wave of the red flag, and every swimmer dove into the water. Daniel was visibly a full second slower to react than the rest. The race had began.

The announcer was keeping up a running commentary over the PA system: "... boy in Lane Two picking up despite his bad start. 25 metres. Lane Three's in the lead, followed by Five.... The race is tightening between Two, Three and Five... 50 meters turnaround... That's a nice turn from Three, Five and Two too." In the stands, there were much cheering for the swimmers – the audience was riveted by the exciting race. Wee Kiang, of course, was yelling for Daniel.

"Lane Two has overtaken Five. Remarkable! He's speeding up, furiously matching up with Three's strokes... But Three's not taking any chance, and still going fast. 75 meters, Five's falling back, with Three and Two barely two meters apart... Will Lane Two catch up? 10 meters more... Three's slowing, Two's up, up... Yes, Two did it!" The crowd roared.

At that moment, Wee Kiang's mother said, "Wee Kiang, look who's here." She motioned for Wee Kiang to turn around. And there she was – his sister – who had seemingly appeared as if by magic and was seated beside their parents, smiling awkwardly. This was the second shock of the day for him. How long had it been since he saw her? Four years. Four long years! He had refused to see her each time she came visiting with his parents, until she gave up. He had bore so much anger and bitterness towards her for so long, and had tried so hard to avoid thinking about her, and had failed.

Now he had finally come face to face with her again and the intense feelings he had expected were, for some unknown reason, no longer there. Instead, he merely felt a strange calmness. But still, he did not know how to react or what to say. For Wee Kiang, Joanne's sudden appearance was probably the hardest thing he ever had to deal with in his life.

Daniel plunged into the water, and he was so mad he felt he could boil the entire pool with his rage. That cad, that traitor Mark, had shown his face! He wanted to cut across the adjacent lanes to catch hold of Mark and choke him, drown him. But his good sense prevailed. Instead, he channeled his anger into one thought – *I must win! I must beat him!* He couldn't bear the thought of coming in worse off than his mortal enemy again. He swam as he had never swam before; he gave it his everything. His entire body seemed to be on fire. And it was only doused when he finally touched the wall. It was only much later, after he had gotten out of the pool immediately and bustled straight to the changing room, that he was informed he had won.

Up in the stands, a family reconciliation was playing out.

"Wee Kiang, you've grown up. I barely can recognise you. I'm sorry that I came late. I've a paper this morning. It's supposed to end at eleven-thirty, but I left the exam hall early to rush here. I'm sorry,

Wee Kiang, for all that happened, but I really miss you. When mum told me about this swimming meet, I know if I don't see you here, we may not meet again until you're…"

"Discharged?" Wee Kiang finally found his voice. "It's ok. I'm used to it now."

"Yes. You've grown a lot," Joanne said, barely above a whisper. "Wee Kiang, I'm sorry about that night. I am very sorry. It was my fault. I caused all this. You shouldn't be here."

"No." Wee Kiang interrupted. "It's not your fault. It's my own. I was petty, immature and selfish. I didn't think so back then, but now, it's so clear to me. I've come to realise many things I didn't before."

Joanne looked at her brother tenderly. He gazed back at her unblinkingly. Then, at the same instant, they smiled at each other. So did their parents, who had been looking on. The chasm between Wee Kiang and Joanne, such a forbidding one, had finally been bridged. The family was, in heart, finally reunited again.

In the changing room, Daniel was sitting by himself and staring into space, stoning. A tentative "Hi Daniel" made him look up.

It was Mark. Yet it wasn't. It was a different Mark. He had lost a lot of weight and looked haggard. Gone too was his swagger and haughtiness – this Mark appeared cowed and defeated, in the way his shoulders slumped and in his dull eyes. He no longer had the confident and gungho aura about him. What had happened to Mark?

"Daniel, I.. I want to say, I am very sorry. I want to.. confess. I framed you that time, and that's why you ended up here. I was jealous of you, and I couldn't accept the reality that you were better. It was a wicked thing to do, I know. And I have beaten myself up about it every single day since. I'm sorry."

In that instant, Daniel felt all the hatred and enmity he had harboured towards Mark leak away, as if it had never existed. This was a strange feeling, but yet it might be comprehensible after all. Wasn't Victor's guilt towards Wai Leng an example? He had went through so much, and Mark too. He didn't want to analyse the whys and whats anymore. He felt unbearably tired, and yet he felt a great weight lifted off his heart.

Daniel looked at Mark again. There was a question he needed to ask.

"How did you land up in this state?"

Mark must have expected this question. He explained without hesitation. "I was caught stealing things from a shop. I guessed the first time I did it was my downfall – it was so easy and nobody caught me. I made it a habit after that. I keep stealing and shoplifting till I was finally caught. Yes, I confess – I stole Coach's money and framed you for it. I'm sorry. But I didn't want to own up to the earlier misdeed. It would have lengthened my time in here, and I wanted to get out as soon as I can. Daniel, I am very sorry."

Everything started to make sense.

Daniel simply said, "Mark, we have suffered enough. Both of us. I don't think I can ever be a friend to you again, at least the way we were. But at least I don't hate you anymore. The past is the past. Let it go."

Without any fuss, he turned away, packed his belongings, and walked out of the changing room, and into a new life.

GRADUATION

For sign language interpreters at the Singapore Association for the Deaf, the journey towards accreditation wasn't easy. Many of them, like Rachel, started off as volunteers with the association, helping out in one activity or another, acquiring proficiency in signing and forging friendships with deaf persons along the way. In the process, they also picked up pointers and knowledge about the deaf and their culture. This form of immersion was fun, stress-free and organic.

Rachel's first encounter with sign language was at a camp for the hearing impaired held by her university's community service club in 1998. She had been totally mesmerised by signing, the way hands and facial expressions took the place of speech. Her interaction with the deaf participants and senior volunteers adept in sign language also inspired her to brush up on her signing.

Rachel joined RSP (HI) in 2001 as a tutor at the Clementi tuition centre. There, she met Joanne who was preparing for her 'A' Level exams. The following year, after seeing her through her As, Rachel took up a sign language interpreting assignment for a Basic Chinese

Course for the Deaf. (Most deaf persons were exempted from second language in school, hence they often had little or no formal instruction in their mother tongue.) That was a challenging assignment; because sign language was a visual language, she had to take note of visual features not intuitive in ordinary communication. This interpreting experience further strengthened her resolve to be a certified interpreter. In late 2002, when SADeaf was recruiting a new batch of interpreters, Rachel decided to give it a shot.

At SADeaf, the word 'interpreter' was usually abbreviated to 'terp'. All aspiring terps had to attend a preparatory workshop, during which trainees were familiarised with the Sign Language Interpreters' Code of Ethics, that is, the dos and don'ts and rights and wrongs of the vocation. Scenarios and settings in which the code apply – such as law courts, job interviews, meetings and hospital consultations – were explained.

At the end of the course, Rachel and her fellow trainees had to undergo 12 months' probation, during which they had to take on at least ten hours of assignments. Real-life interpreting was more than just signing, as Rachel learnt. The speed of interpretation and signing using the native grammar of the deaf become key. Sign language as used by the deaf is not English as it is written or spoken, but has a grammar and syntax of its own more suited to the spatial and visual nature of the language. This is something good terps pick up and employ during assignments. Other challenges a terp had to overcome include stage fright (especially for assignments on an actual stage and in front of a large audience), ensuring good lighting to be clearly visible to the clients, ignoring curious stares, battling bodily and mental fatigue, among others. It was particularly draining when interpreting during meetings in which speakers spoke over and interrupted one another.

Still, most terps find their work rewarding and fulfilling; they know they are rendering an important service which enables their deaf clients to have full and equal access to communication and information.

The convocation ceremony fell on 14 September. In a full-length blue gown, a light blue sash hanging from her broad shoulders and a mortarboard on her head, Joanne stood smartly in line at the side of the auditorium, waiting for her turn on stage. Her heart was beating furiously, her eyes glancing around. But she was not looking at anyone in particular. She was just trying to work off the nervousness engulfing her. Yes, she was overjoyed to have come so far, but at the same time, felt matter-of-fact about it.

Joanne looked at Rachel and noticed she, too, was a bit jittery, probably because she was interpreting on stage. Most interpreters would be unless they were really seasoned. And for this event, the President of Singapore was on stage! Rachel finally signed her name, and her legs seemed to move automatically up the short flight of steps and onto the stage, and twenty odd paces more towards the president, who shook her hand, presented a scroll and a silver plaque engraved with the words 'EEE Outstanding Student Award', turned to face the photographer and smiled as the flash went off.

That was it! The convocation. Over in less than half a minute.

To Huifen, the moment was as magical to her as it was for Joanne. And Joanne's results were not surprising to Huifen. Second Upper was a given, considering her mettle and brain prowess. She was not the only local deaf graduate of course; NUS boasted its first in 1991 while NTU's first was in 1995. Subsequently, there were a few more from each university, but all were males. This meant Joanne was the first female local graduate, a landmark achievement by any measure. Huifen hoped that Mr and Mrs Chua understood what their daughter's achievements really meant.

After the ceremony, Joanne was approached by a group of media and TV folks outside the auditorium. They requested for an interview about her educational journey in NTU. Joanne was game. "Sure. Why not? I'm honoured."

"Ms Chua, first of all, please accept our thanks for granting us this opportunity for an interview with you. As we know, you're the first female hearing-impaired graduate from the Nanyang Technological University. We'd indeed be honoured to learn about some of your experiences. How do you feel about having graduated?"

"Overwhelmed! Unexpected! Disbelief, then euphoria! Actually, no words can describe what I am feeling now... it is simply a special and amazing feeling. I never expected to come this far, to be honest. The first thing I will do is to hug my family, especially my parents who had never given up on me." She pointed at Mr and Mrs Chua, who were standing nearby and beaming proudly.

"Joanne, in view of your disability, do you feel a greater sense of achievement because of the barriers you had to overcome?"

This made Joanne pause. Then she said, "It was a challenge, no doubt. In some ways, it was more difficult for me, I guess. I feel

I had to work twice as hard as others because of my hearing loss. That's all. But to your question, no. I feel I have achieved a lot and am proud of myself. But it's not a greater achievement than my fellow graduates because I think all of them went through the same hardship to graduate today too."

"You mentioned the only thing you ask for is being accepted for who you are. Do you think enough is being done for the deaf in Singapore?"

"There was some progress over the past few years, thanks to the VWO and many volunteers groups and the VWO's efforts. But much more is needed, for example subtitling is needed on TV programmes during major national events. I think deafness is the most commonly known about disability but the least understood. For example, many people, even doctors, don't know the deaf can listen and speak and the term 'deaf and mute' is often wrongly used to describe the deaf. They also may not realise there is quite a number of highly qualified executives in the IT and engineering lines who are deaf, or that some deaf people can speak well and even sing beautifully."

"So you think society should play a more active role to integrate the deaf? How can we do that?"

"That's where public education comes in. Some adjustments are also necessary; for example, I needed tutors and classmates to take turns to speak and to speak clearly when I am in the group. But above all, the deaf must themselves make the effort. They must know they can do it. Wherever possible, they should adopt auditory rehabilitation to help them listen better with their hearing aids, and thereafter acquire language and speech. Only when the deaf person attempts to listen and speak, and the hearing public attempts to understand, will the gap between us be fully bridged."

"What message do you have for all those deaf kids in their academic pursuit?"

Joanne did not hesitate. She replied instantly, "Helen Keller once said, 'Blindness cuts you off from things, deafness cuts you off from people.' That is the greatest challenge for all of us, to win back people and society, through overcoming our deafness. If we only sign, we will forever be in our own world. That is the case in the States. But they have a big 'own world' over there, a few-million-strong community. We can sign, and that's important to retain our undeniable identity as a deaf person, but we should also be forward looking and unyielding in improving our hearing so that we're not cut off from society. A whole generation before us has not broken out of that norm. Let's not lose another generation."

"That's good advice, Joanne. Now I'm sure you'd like to thank some people in your life as well."

"Of course. I am very grateful to my tutors from NTU for their patience and confidence in me, my good 'sister' Huifen who had shared in my joys and sorrows, my wonderful parents, and the one last person to whom I owe my success most – Wee Kiang, my younger brother. Without his beautiful singing, I would not have realised music is heaven to one's ears, and without his pursuit for his 'O' Level exams in the toughest of situations, I would never have striven hard enough to finish my degree this year."

"Wee Kiang, today's also the happiest day of my life because it's both our graduations. It's a dream come true."

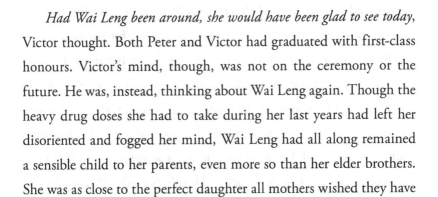

Had Wai Leng been around, she would have been glad to see today, Victor thought. Both Peter and Victor had graduated with first-class honours. Victor's mind, though, was not on the ceremony or the future. He was, instead, thinking about Wai Leng again. Though the heavy drug doses she had to take during her last years had left her disoriented and fogged her mind, Wai Leng had all along remained a sensible child to her parents, even more so than her elder brothers. She was as close to the perfect daughter all mothers wished they have could be, and almost the perfect sister too. She could be counted on to do the right thing and conduct herself the right way as well.

Those who knew the family well would also concur the youngest child was also the wisest. Mother would recount fondly the many stories about Wai Leng from their childhood, incidents blurred by the passage of time but which would remain forever vivid in her memories. Such as when eight-year-old Wai Leng sneaked out alone to buy a Mother's Day gift of a necklace with her piggy bank savings, and how, a year later, she had told Dad she would buy him a packet of cigarettes a month when she started earning money. Wai Leng was still healthy then, but she was beginning to be aware of her condition. Sometimes, she would take out the photos of herself as a toddler and ask why she was not as plump as before. When she was ten, she asked a very flustered Mother if she would "grow up normal like other kids."

The first sign of trouble occurred when she was in primary six, and the doctor advised her to "take it easy" with her studies, so she repeated the year. She had the good fortune to have sympathetic teachers and a kind principal. In the end, she scored 183 points for PSLE, and was placed in the Normal (Technical) Stream in a neighbourhood secondary school. But her condition took a turn for the worse, and she had to drop out of school that year. She was only fifteen then, Yet she had to contend with the devastating knowledge that she had no more goals and no hope for the future. Wai Leng was stoic and strong for a time, but the strain was too much for her in the end as her mind and spirit crumpled. But what she could not achieve herself, Wai Leng hoped her two academically-inclined brothers could. When they did well in their PSLE and Os, Wai Leng was so happy she bought supper for them to celebrate.

It was a joyful occasion for the family. Dad and Mum were in their best attire and Peter even borrowed a gown from a studio so he and Victor looked like fellow top students instead of brothers four years apart. They all felt blessed they had finally reconciled as a family.

Victor had found it in him to forgive his father. The old man had slipped into coma one night due to low blood sugar. Alone at home with his father, Victor single-handedly tried to revive him and was terrified that would be the last he saw of his old man. He hugged him and shook him hard, crying at the same time. Was he going to lose him forever? The thought they would part forever on a bitter note of enmity was a sobering one. His father eventually recovered and Victor likewise developed a new perspective on how fleeting life was and to let go of past hurts.

Then, one evening, he confided to Mother, for the first time, about his persistent sense of guilt towards Wai Leng all those years. "But Wai Leng never blamed you or Peter," she replied. "A few weeks before her passing, she suddenly asked me if two of you ever felt bad for mistreating her. I said I don't think so, she's just being too sensitive and shouldn't worry. But she told me she doesn't blame any of you at all. She said she knew she was being irritating at times, and as her brother, you were right to teach her a lesson when she got out of hand. Anyhow, she told me the physical pain we inflicted on her was nothing at all compared to her torment when her condition acted up, so we really don't have to feel guilty."

Mother's concluding words on this also stayed with him: "Wai Leng is like a child of Heaven. She seemed to sense the end was near and told me the day before she passed on, 'Don't worry Ma, Brother and Victor will take good care of you forever. They are good brothers and good people, so they will.'"

Upon hearing this, Victor wept. Like a condemned prisoner receiving the mercy of God and a new lease of life, he had realised his guilt was unfounded all along. He had been a good brother in the eyes of his sister, and he had been entrusted to take care of his mother simply because his sister had faith in him.

AFTERWORD

I am heartened that my journey to get this book published has borne fruit after more than a decade. The book captures some of my volunteering experiences from 1995 to 2008, which have been etched into my long-term memory, in print so that I can share them with a wider audience.

The *esprit de coup* among volunteers and the roller-coaster emotions they experience when working with needy clients, is a world in stark contrast to metropolitan city life. At first, at the beginning of my stint, I had thought I was helping these special needs beneficiaries, but instead, I found that I had also gained much in being exposed to life-changing perspectives and character-building insights.

Since my initial work on this manuscript in 2004, Singapore's social service scene has been transformed tremendously as we seek to build an inclusive society in which no one is left behind. The restructuring of the Ministry of Community, Youth and Sports (MCYS) to become two separate entities – the Ministry of Social and Family Development (MSF) and the Ministry of Culture, Community and Youth (MCCY) in 2014 – shows how much attention the government is now devoting to the social service sector. The establishment of a dedicated training and employment-focused agency for persons with disabilities in the form of SG Enable, as well as improvements in disability-friendly transport and access are some of the significant moves towards greater integration in the decade since. Most recently, the Ministry of Education took another big step by extending compulsory education to children with disabilities. Singapore also came together as one to cheer our Paralympians, including gold medalist Yip Ping Xiu, who have demonstrated extraordinary resilience and tenacity, and showed non-disabled persons that disability is not inability.

While the government is to be commended for taking the lead, there is much more to do at the community and individual levels in terms of changing mindsets and integrating our disabled and special needs community more fully. We have a long way to go in addressing issues of discrimination and prejudice, along with other current social woes such as xenophobia and a growing rich-poor divide. The fight continues, and so we must stay the course.

I hope the simple stories in this book inspire more people to take up the gauntlet. We all can do our part to ensure that these historically marginalised and overlooked segments of society are not left behind as we march on towards Singapore's vision of SG100.

Thank you for supporting the cause of *Three Gems*.

God bless,

Derek Liang

December 2016

Printed in the United States
By Bookmasters